STEVE JACKSON   IAN LIVINGSTONE

FIGHTING FANTASY

GATES
OF
DEATH

CHARLIE

Fighting Fantasy: dare you play them all?

THE

GATES

OF

DEATH

CHARLIE HIGSON

■SCHOLASTIC

Scholastic Children's Books
An imprint of Scholastic Ltd
Euston House, 24 Eversholt Street, London, NW1 1DB, UK
Registered office: Westfield Road, Southam, Warwickshire, CV47 0RA
SCHOLASTIC and associated logos are trademarks and/or
registered trademarks of Scholastic Inc.

First published in the UK by Scholastic Ltd, 2018

Text and illustration copyright © Ian Livingstone and Steve Jackson, 2018
Written by Charlie Higson
Cover illustration by Robert Ball
Inside illustrations by Vlado Krizan
Map illustration by Leo Hartas

Fighting Fantasy is a trademark owned by Steve Jackson
and Ian Livingstone, all rights reserved

ISBN 978 1407 18630 6

A CIP catalogue record for this book
is available from the British Library.

Printed by CPI Group (UK) Ltd, Croydon, CR0 4YY
Papers used by Scholastic Children's Books are made
from wood grown in sustainable forests.

This ~~book is a work of fiction. Names, characters, places, incidents~~
and di~~alogues are products of the author's imagination, or are used~~
fict~~itiously. Any resemblance to actual people, living or dead,~~
~~events or locales is entirely coincidental.~~

CONTENTS

HOW WILL YOU START YOUR ADVENTURE?

The book you hold in your hands is a gateway to another world – a world of dark magic, terrifying monsters, brooding castles, treacherous dungeons and untold danger, where a noble few defend against the myriad schemes of the forces of evil. Welcome to the world of **FIGHTING FANTASY!**

You are about to embark upon a thrilling fantasy adventure in which **YOU** are the hero! **YOU** decide which route to take, which dangers to risk and which creatures to fight. But be warned – it will also be **YOU** who has to live or die by the consequences of your actions.

Take heed, for success is by no means certain, and you may well fail in your mission on your first attempt. But have no fear, for with experience, skill and luck, each new attempt should bring you a step closer to your ultimate goal.

Prepare yourself, for when you turn the page you will enter an exciting, perilous **FIGHTING FANTASY** adventure where every choice is yours to make, an adventure in which **YOU ARE THE HERO!**

How would you like to begin your adventure?

IF YOU ARE NEW TO FIGHTING FANTASY ...

It's a good idea to read the rules before you start, which appear on pages 329-338.

IF YOU HAVE PLAYED FIGHTING FANTASY BEFORE ...

You'll realize that to have any chance of success, you will need to discover your hero's attributes. You can create your own character by following the instructions on pages 329-330. Don't forget to enter your character's details on the Adventure Sheet which appears on pages 340-341.

Please also take note of the updated rules regarding provisions and the new rules regarding weapons that appear on pages 333-338.

ALTERNATIVE DICE

If you do not have a pair of dice handy, dice rolls are printed throughout the book at the bottom of the pages. Flicking rapidly through the book and stopping on a page will give you a random dice roll. If you need to 'roll' only one die, read only the first printed die; if two, total the two dice symbols.

BACKGROUND

The Crucible Isles lie in the southern stretches of the great Western Ocean, shrouded in mist and ringed by dangerous rocks. Few outsiders venture here, but those that do are welcomed by the ancient Guardians of the Crucible and taught the healing arts. In time they will learn how to create magic potions in the giant stone crucible that gives the islands their name. If they have the skill they might attain the level of Guardian, dedicated to tending the Great Crucible.

The islands are quiet, and very little happens here, but one day the calm is broken by the arrival of a desperate messenger from Allansia.

'I bring terrible news,' he says when he is taken to the Great High Guardian in the Chapter Hall. 'A plague has broken out in Allansia. People who are struck down by the sickness are turning into hideous, demonic monsters.'

'So,' says the Great High Guardian, her face clouded with worry. 'The demon plague has returned. If it is allowed to spread it will eventually infect every inhabitant of Titan.

There is a cure, however: smoke-oil, distilled from the roots of the Asura Lily. We have a small supply here, not enough to cure more than a hundred people, but if we were to take some of it to the Temple of Throff in Allansia, the High Priestess there might be able to use her magic skills to produce enough to save everyone. There is one problem, though; for its own protection, the temple is hidden within the Invisible City...'

It is the season of storms and high seas, but there is no time to lose, and so a small band of Guardians sets sail from the Crucible Isles, headed for Allansia with sixty vials of smoke-oil. You are only a humble acolyte, still learning your skills, but it is your duty to serve Brother Tobyn, one of the Guardians, and so you travel with him.

'We will land in Kaynlesh-Ma, in south-west Allansia, where the people are famous for their wisdom,' Brother Tobyn explains as the Crucible Isles disappear over the horizon. 'We are sure that someone there will be able to tell us how to find the Invisible City.'

But the Gods have other plans for you.

The seas are dangerous, lashed by tempests and furious winds, infested with pirates and monsters of the deep. When you finally make land in Allansia, it is not at the peaceful harbour of Kaynlesh-Ma, but somewhere very different indeed.

YOUR ADVENTURE AWAITS!

May your STAMINA never fail!

NOW TURN OVER...

You step up on to the gangplank and walk down to the dockside. It feels good to have solid ground beneath your feet after being so long at sea, although you feel wobbly and unstable and are very sick from the voyage. You kneel down, intending to kiss dry land and instead you heave up your last meal on to the cobblestones. (Lose 5 *STAMINA* points.)

At least you are alive, though. You feared you would not survive the voyage. Your tiny fleet was blown way off course, and six days ago the last surviving ships were wrecked and you were flung into the icy ocean. It was only by some miracle that you and Brother Tobyn were snared in the nets of a fishing boat, whose captain dragged you out of the water and brought you here, to Port Blacksand. Of all the people who set off from the Crucible Isles, you and Brother Tobyn are the only two left.

You turn to help your master down the gangplank. Brother Tobyn, who is old and bald and stooped, is sick from spending so long in the water after the wreck. His legs shake and he holds out an arm so that you can steady him.

'We've made it, then,' he says and offers up a prayer of thanks to Throff. He then passes you the last surviving vials of smoke-oil for safekeeping.

'There are only ten,' he says. 'Guard them well. I wish we had more, but if we can only get one vial to the High Priestess in the Invisible City, we will have succeeded. Now, we must get out of Port Blacksand as quickly as possible. This does not look a friendly place at all...'

He's right. The narrow winding streets that lead away from the harbour are dark and dirty, with crumbling buildings overhanging them, and in some cases meeting at the top. The dockside is crowded with a variety of unwashed people who look like they're adding to the general stink of rotting fish and sewage that hangs in the air. You see traders and sailors, adventurers, pirates, men for hire, beggars and shady characters of all types.

'We must eat before we do anything else,' says Brother Tobyn, and you follow your noses away from the wharf and up Catfish Street to the Fish Market. The market is situated in a busy square, where you find a fishwife grilling sardines over hot coals. The smell of her cooking jabs like a knife at your empty belly.

As you make your way over to the fishwife, you pass a stall selling fishing equipment, hooks and anchors, nets, belaying pins and even a couple of whaling harpoons.

The fishwife tells you it will be 1 Gold Piece for a meal.

Making sure nobody is looking, you pull your purse out from where it's hidden in the folds of your tunic and count your money. You only have 10 Gold Pieces and the price is criminal, but you're desperate to eat. If you want to pay the woman, turn to **18**. If you refuse her price, turn to **32**.

2

You move away from the dead soldiers, not wanting to see them as they turn back into ordinary men.

'Well done!' shouts Lady Webspinn, pointing towards a doorway. 'Now hurry! Find Swann!'

You don't need to be told twice. You run from the Halls of Learning and on to a landing lined with more books. Turn to **15**.

3

Working quickly, you jiggle the fishhook in the lock until you feel it snap open. Slowly you pull the door back. Turn to **130**.

4

You ride hard, not even risking stopping for food, following the horse's lead, and arrive at Salamonis as the sun is dipping in the sky. Turn to **446**.

5

You're more confident than before and thrust your hand quickly into the hole. Something pricks your finger, but it doesn't hurt too much and you keep searching until you have hold of something metal. You pull it out and see that it's an assassin's stiletto knife. There's a tiny drop of blood on the needle-like tip of the blade – your blood. So it was this blade that pricked you. You smile and suck your finger. This dagger might come in useful. But as you try to stand up you start to feel sick and light-headed.

It's then that you remember assassins often poison their blades.

If you have any poison antidote, turn to **24**. If not, turn to **44**.

6

As you reach for the smoke-oil, the dungeon-master gives a howl of delight and snatches it away from you.

'That's too precious for the likes of you,' he cackles. 'I'm saving this for Lord Azzur. You're on your own...'

The dungeon-master giggles as Brother Tobyn claws at you, shredding your sleeve and drawing blood from your arm. Lose 2 *STAMINA* points. To take the rusty bread knife, turn to **26**. To fight DEMON BROTHER TOBYN with your bare hands, turn to **53**.

7

You walk all around the cavern but don't find anything you haven't seen before. To try the rings hanging from the gates, turn to **356**. To investigate the fresh body, turn to **193**. To leave the cavern and go back up to the refectory, turn to **460.**

8

You walk along the track, which curves away from the settlement to the north. You can hardly see anything in the gathering darkness but you hear a buzzing sound and then feel a sharp sting on your arm. Soon a swarm of biting flies surrounds you. (Lose 1 *STAMINA* point.) To hurry on, turn to **39**. To run back the way you came, turn to **408**.

9

You grab a vial of smoke-oil from your pack and hurl it to the ground. It smashes and a cloud of yellow gas swamps the thieves. They cough and splutter and wipe their eyes. But it hasn't harmed them, only made them very angry indeed. It seems that smoke-oil is only effective against demons.

Cross one vial of smoke-oil off your Adventure Sheet and then turn to **218.**

You catch the glint of a smile

10

You pop the cork from the bottle of 'Nostalgia' and a pink gas that smells of pears wafts out. You feel your whole world spinning... Time seems to run backwards... You realize the potion will allow you to relive part of your adventure... Turn to **466.**

11

You walk on a little way down the road but stop as you hear the noise of thundering hooves behind you. You turn to see four black horses pulling a black carriage bearing down on you from the direction of Port Blacksand. You jump out of the road to avoid being run down, but the driver pulls on the reins and the carriage stops beside you in a cloud of dust.

An elegant-looking lady leans out of the window, her face covered by a veil. You catch the glint of a smile.

'Thank you so much,' she says. 'Those highway robbers have been stopping all traffic on this road and stealing from honest travellers. You've dealt with them once and for all. I can offer you a ride in my carriage. My name is Lady Webspinn and I am going to Salamonis. If you're headed that way, why don't you climb aboard...?'

If you want to take up Lady Webspinn's offer, turn to **61.** If you want to refuse it, turn to **41.**

12

You go over to the Pool of Miseries, look into the water and feel suddenly tired. You want to fall into the water, sink into its depths and sleep for ever. Instead, you drink some water from it and suddenly feel weak and ill. (Lose 1 *STAMINA* point.)

To go north down the Walkway of Night, turn to **406**. To go south down the Walkway of Evening, turn to **84**.

13

You climb over the fallen pillar and, as you slide down the other side, the cracked paving gives way beneath your feet. You are falling into the sewers. Turn to **330**.

14

If you have any of the following items listed on your Adventure Sheet, cross them off now:

Poison Antidote, Sneaky Sword, Pitchfork, Assassin's Stiletto, Woodman's Axe, Book of Love Poetry, Fire Iron, Jewelled Warhammer, Harp of Healing.

(Your Provisions, Gold Pieces, any potions and vials of smoke-oil are unaffected by the strange magic.)

Restore your *SKILL*, *STAMINA* and *LUCK* scores to their Initial values and turn to **100**.

15

You leap down a sweeping marble staircase and across an entrance hall before bursting outside, just as the clouds open and dump a deluge of purple rain on to the city. Turn to **167**.

16

If you are wearing the swift boots, turn to **46**. If not then turn to **31**.

17

You gallop on through the night, wondering where the sure-footed horse will take you. As the hours pass you doze off in the saddle. (Add 2 *STAMINA* points.) You are eventually woken with a start by a noise like thunder in time to see a familiar black carriage go rattling past you in a cloud of dust.

You look at the position of the sun and figure that you must have ridden all night and most of the following day. You find that you are still sitting on the horse's back, and it has stopped to crop some grass by a river that passes below some high city walls. From what Brother Tobyn told you, you think this must be Salamonis, famous for its ancient walls. Turn to **446**.

18

The fishwife takes your money and you and Brother Tobyn share some sardines.

Add 2 *STAMINA* points, deduct 1 Gold Piece from your total, and turn to **32**.

19

'You are a rotten bully,' says the King of Imps. 'But if you kill us, we all die!' So saying, he pulls what looks like a small cannonball with a fuse sticking out of it from under his tunic. He lights it from one of the fire pots and, before you can stop him, he hurls it at the funeral bier. Turn to **62**.

20

'Ah, so you want to see my equipment for explorers,' says Swann, leading you over to some shelves. 'I have these magical silver swift boots; for only 6 Gold Pieces they will get you quickly past any danger. Very useful on the streets of Salamonis right now, I'd say. Also, I have this silver compass, cheap at 5 Gold Pieces; the adventurer who was here bought one just like it, said it was just what he needed. Or what about this stylish sun hat, only 8 Gold Pieces? Or this stout walking staff for only 10 Gold Pieces?'

You can sense that Swann is desperate. The prices are far too high for these ordinary objects. But buy anything you want, and can afford, put on any clothing you've bought and then turn to **364**.

Even though you are inside the city and walking its streets, the buildings appear to shimmer and wobble like a mirage, occasionally becoming transparent as if the whole place might disappear again at any moment. The city has no outer walls. Its defence is its invisibility. Far above you, you can see the silver dome of the Great Temple of Throff that dominates the place. Clustered around the main temple are the domes and spires of lesser temples and religious buildings. You can also see several tall columns with statues on them, looking out across the plains, and long banners flapping from poles, orange and red and yellow.

All the roads in the city lead up to the temple, winding around the rock, climbing ever steeper to the summit through hanging gardens. There are bridges, archways and viaducts all the way up, roads on top of roads, so that the city resembles a giant tower. Down here on the lower levels you can see public buildings, shops and taverns and houses, but the temple dominates. The population can't be very large. It would be hard to sustain too many people in such a barren place, and most of the inhabitants presumably serve the temple, but even so – where is everybody? The streets are deserted. It is as if you've wandered into a ghost town.

To explore the lower levels, turn to **34**. To climb immediately to the Great Temple, turn to **131**.

22

It takes several blows to chop through the door and on the last swing the shaft snaps. You throw the axe away and open the door.

Cross the axe off your Adventure Sheet and turn to **130**.

23

You walk along the track, which snakes round to the west. As you pick your way through the darkness you hear a buzzing sound and then feel a sharp sting on your neck. Soon a swarm of biting flies surrounds you. (Lose 1 *STAMINA* point.) To hurry on, turn to **39**. To run back the way you came, turn to **408**.

24

You use your antidote. (Remove it from your Adventure Sheet.) You are safe this time. (Add the assassin's stiletto to your Weapons List.)

To go back to the stable, turn to **401**. To go into the inn, turn to **361**.

25

You rush forward, your khopesh catching the weird light from the flames and sending shards of colour all around the walls of the cavern. You hack your way through the front rank of demons. Your khopesh is mightily powerful here, but not powerful enough to defeat a whole army. You realize that without any more magic you have no chance.

Ulrakaah urges her army on. She's stooped over, with a back bent like an old crone, but she lifts her two massive swords with ease and roars again.

'Ulrakaaaah!'

And the demonic army echoes her as they charge forward like a tide of filth and roll over you. The last thing you see before darkness overwhelms you is one of Ulrakaah's swords slashing down through the fetid air to slice you in two.

You know your adventure is surely over. Turn to **60.**

26

You grab the rusty bread knife and turn around just in time to confront the demon. It's going to be a tough fight but you might just have a chance. Brother Tobyn was old and weak and so is the demon he's become. Add the rusty bread knife to your Weapons List and turn to **53.**

27

'I'm growing faint,' says the man, the chains slipping through his sweaty palms. 'This is your last chance...' Turn to **444**.

28

You walk carefully down the street, alert to any danger. There has been a battle here and dead bodies lie all around. A fine old building has been pulled down, spilling rubble into the street, and a fallen pillar blocks your way. To go back the way you came, turn to **128**. To climb over the pillar, turn to **13**.

29

You pull the cork out of the bottle labelled 'Thick as Thieves' and nasty blue smoke wafts out. You cover your mouth and nose and drop the bottle. The smoke seems to be alive. It seeks out the thieving Highwaymen and they can't help but breathe it in.

A dim look comes into their eyes. They stand there blinking and confused, not sure where they are, or even who they are.

'Who's this bloke, then?' says one, peering at you. 'Is it Lord Azzur?'

'Don't be stupid,' says another. 'Lord Azzur's much taller than that.'

'Don't you call me stupid! How d'you know how tall he is? You ever seen him?'

'I saw a dead frog once.'

'What's that got to do with anything, you idiot?'

'Are you calling me an idiot?'

'I think so, yeah...'

'Say it again, cabbage brain, and I'll hit you with this whatchamacallit?' says the second highwayman, raising his sword.

'It's a, erm, a mop, I think...' says a third.

'A mop, you berk? It's a sausage... No, it's a...'

'You're all fools. It's a cucumber... No... Er...'

'Yeah, well I'll show you what it does!'

In a moment they've all started fighting each other, and not long after that they all lie dead in the road. Turn to **262.**

30

You put some dried fish in the bowl and send a prayer to Lunara to help you find the priestess. Nothing happens. Turn to **406.**

31

You walk on until you come to the East Gate, but instantly see that there's no chance of getting out of the city this way. The gates are on fire and at least twenty demons are dancing around waving flaming torches. You turn and run back towards Titan Square before they see you. Turn to **149.**

It strikes Brother Tobyn down

32

'Put your purse away,' says Brother Tobyn, pushing your hand back inside your tunic. You wonder what the problem is and then see that two men are arguing nearby. One of them is Heathcote, the captain of the fishing boat that rescued you. He's still dressed in his waterproof, weather-beaten leathers. The other man is a local merchant, wealthy, by the look of him, with jewelled rings on his fingers and a large gold medallion hanging on his chest.

'You're no better than the thieves and cutthroats who infest this place,' Heathcote shouts, grabbing a handful of the merchant's fine silk robes. 'The price you're offering me for my catch is robbery, plain and simple.'

'It's the best price you'll get in Port Blacksand,' says the merchant. 'Believe me.'

'I nearly died catching those fish,' says Captain Heathcote. 'I was warned about this place. But, because of the storms, it was the only place we could put in.'

People are starting to gather round, some taking Captain Heathcote's side, some taking the side of the merchant, who is shaking and getting very red in the face. You see that foam is forming around his mouth and his eyes are losing their focus. And then suddenly he snarls and tries to bite Captain Heathcote, who jumps back in surprise.

The next moment the merchant bends over double, his back cracking and popping. When he straightens up, you see that the whites of his eyes have gone dark and his teeth appear to have grown bigger and sharper. Even as you watch, his skin turns rough and warty and his fingernails grow into long claws. There are screams as people back away.

'It's the plague!' someone shouts. 'The plague has come to Port Blacksand. He has the demon curse!'

The thing that was once the merchant lashes out with awful strength, sending Captain Heathcote flying.

'Stop!' Brother Tobyn cries out, raising both arms. 'I command you to stop!'

But now the DEMON MERCHANT has seen him. It turns its dark eyes on him and advances. Before you can do anything, it strikes Brother Tobyn down. You see that he has been wounded but is mercifully still alive. A group of locals draw their weapons, but they hang back, scared. If you don't do something fast, the demon is going to attack your master again.

'Remember,' gasps Brother Tobyn, 'our mission is to help

the people of Allansia and rid them of the demon plague...'

If you want to grab the Guardian and try to make a run for it, turn to **56**. If you want to try to attack the Demon Merchant, turn to **77**. If you want to use one of the precious vials of smoke-oil to try to cure the Demon Merchant, turn to **107**.

33

You raise your weapon and bear down on the Imps, yelling a battle cry. Most of them run off screaming, but five remain, including their king. You could easily beat them now. To carry on with your attack, turn to **19**. To talk to them, turn to **142**.

34

The longer you spend in the city, the more solid it seems to become. Among the houses on the lower slopes you find a clothworks, with weaving equipment, dyeing vats, and cutting and sewing rooms. Next door to it is a maker of scientific equipment and then a pottery. On the next street you find a tavern. Most of the buildings have blue-tiled roofs, but many have gardens growing on them where food crops are mixed in among the flowers. You see some bushes heavy with bean pods on top of a two-storey house opposite the tavern.

To climb up on to the roof, turn to **52**. To enter the tavern, turn to **86**. To carry on up towards the temple, turn to **131**.

35

You grab a vial of smoke-oil from your pack and hurl it at the soldiers. It hits the first one on the breastplate and smashes, enveloping them both in gas. They collapse, coughing and spluttering, with smoke streaming from their mouths.

Soon they have recovered, and look around, confused and scared. Then they go over to the scholars.

'We will protect you,' they say and you are able to hurry from the Halls of Learning to look for a way out of the building. Turn to **15.**

36

'Ah, yes, I do have a few jars of magic potion left, and even some perfume,' says Swann. 'Take your pick, only 5 Gold Pieces each.'

Swann offers you a jar of 'Thick as Thieves', a jar of 'Pretty as a Picture', a jar of 'Dragon's Breath', a jar of 'Collywobbles' and a bottle of 'Nostalgia' perfume.

Deduct 5 Gold Pieces for each one you buy and turn to **364.**

37

You gallop on through the night, hoping that you are heading in the right direction. The hours pass and you keep dozing off in the saddle. At last, though, you see some buildings up ahead and urge the horse towards them.

It seems to take for ever, but eventually you arrive on the outskirts of a town. The houses look well-built and the streets are clean and wide, and there's the welcoming sign of an inn – The Old Toad. This must be Silverton. You dismount and let the horse head back to the woods. It's still raining and you take a look around. Turn to **254**.

38

You are in a large six-sided chamber with a pool of dark water in the middle. The Walkway of Night leads north to the main temple. The red-tiled Walkway of Evening leads south. This is the famous Pool of Miseries, one of two magical pools here in the temple that you learnt about from Brother Tobyn on the voyage from the Crucible Isles. The walls glow and shimmer as if lit by moonlight. You feel suddenly tired and gloomy and you can't remember if it's day or night.

To drink some water from the pool, turn to **12**. To go north down the Walkway of Night, turn to **406**. To go south down the Walkway of Evening, turn to **84**.

39

You sprint on along the track and at last manage to outrun the flies (but not before losing 1 more *STAMINA* point). Soon, up ahead of you, you see the watchtower and realize that this foraging track must join up with the other one. Turn to **408**.

40

You ride in front of the black carriage and hail the driver. He hauls on the reins and the carriage judders to a halt.

'You're blocking the road, you dirty tramp,' says the driver. 'Lady Webspinn is in a hurry to get to Salamonis.'

Now that you know which way to go, do you want to let the carriage drive on? If so, turn to **180**. Or, if you want to talk to Lady Webspinn, turn to **139**.

41

'Very well,' says the elegant lady. 'But this is a dangerous road, and the way to the next town is long and hard. Good luck.' So saying she shouts to the driver and the carriage rattles away.

Maybe it'll be safer away from the road. You walk through some tall grass, climb over a fence into a cornfield and then find an old herders' track that will take you cross-country. Turn to **159**.

42

Your khopesh is too powerful for the demon queen, and you strike her dead. Her last cry of 'Ulrakaaaah!' echoes around the cavern as her body collapses and dissolves into a pool of purple slime. You slump down on to a rock, exhausted, relieved that it is over at last. You have defeated the demon queen and her army, but now you realize that you are trapped here, in her realm, for ever. You did it by using her own dark power against her, and you look at the khopesh in your hand. You know how dangerous it is, the dark power it holds. You force yourself to stand and walk over to the fiery pit.

You look down at the flames. To drop the khopesh in, turn to **201**. To keep hold of it, just in case, turn to **400**.

43

'Do not go to Salamonis,' says the Lamassu. 'I know I said I would take you anywhere, but I will never go back there. Its streets are filled with demons. There are only a few people left who are unaffected by the curse, and there are demon portals on every street corner that will suck you into oblivion. If you do insist on going there, there is one man who could help you. His name is Sandford Swann and he is a mapmaker. Stay on the main streets and if you can make it to Titan Square you need to take the road that heads north and then the second street on the left.'

To ask the Lamassu about the Invisible City, turn to **59**. To thank the Lamassu and continue to Salamonis on horseback, turn to **240**. To fly past Salamonis on the Lamassu, turn to **463**.

44

Maybe there wasn't enough poison left on the blade to kill you. *Test your Luck.*

If you are Lucky, turn to **66**. If you are Unlucky, turn to **87**.

45

'Hurry,' says the man. 'Do something! I can't hold on to these damned dogs much longer...' Turn to **444**.

46

You are racing down the East Road towards the city gates. Glancing over your shoulder you see that the Demon Horde is catching up with you. It looks like you've picked up every demon in Salamonis, too many to count. At their head is a demon wearing expensive robes and a golden crown. You realize this must be King Salamon himself. Not even he could escape the demon curse.

The noise they make is like a herd of cattle, moaning and grunting, their feet pounding on the cobblestones. You push yourself to run faster, and with the swift boots on your feet, you feel as if you are almost flying.

Now you see the gatehouse ahead of you. It's been scorched by fire and the gates themselves have burnt down. Several dead citizens are scattered on the ground and a unit of five tired and bloody soldiers stands guard.

You spot Lady Webspinn's carriage, ready to leave, with its four black horses harnessed to the traces. There's no sign of the driver or Lady Webspinn anywhere, however.

To stop running and look inside the carriage, turn to **58**. To make a run for it towards the gates, turn to **216**. To ask the soldiers to help you fight the Demon Horde, turn to **207**.

47

It takes several blows to smash the lock with the fire iron, and as it finally gives way you hear a shout behind you.

'Oi! What d'you think you're playing at?'

The noise has alerted FOSSICK, who stands there brandishing his big woodsman's axe. This time you're going to have to fight him.

Choose a weapon from your list and prepare to fight. If you have no weapon you will have to use the fire iron.

FOSSICK   *SKILL 8*   *STAMINA 9*

If you win, turn to **68**.

48

The Imps scream and fall back as the clay pot smashes and fire spills out in all directions. But the next moment there's a great WHOOMPH! and the liquid in the basin is burning fiercely. If you have a flask of firewater, turn to **76**. If not, turn to **62**.

49

You pull the cork out of the bottle labelled 'Pretty as a Picture' and a cloud of turquoise gas escapes. It smells of lavender. The Highwaymen cough and choke. They are weakened but still alive. (Deduct 3 from each one's *STAMINA*.)

If the Highwaymen have lost all their *STAMINA*, turn to **262**. If the Highwaymen still have some *STAMINA*, turn to **218**.

50

You walk down the street. There are fires burning inside some of the buildings. Smoke fills the road. You walk through it and the next thing you know you are falling. You have stepped into a demon portal and are sinking into a pool of purple ectoplasm. Turn to **355**.

51

You just manage to push past the Demon Soldiers and get to the door. You hear shouts and screams behind you but ignore them and carry on running. You realize, though, that one of the soldiers has scratched you.

Lose 2 *STAMINA* points and turn to **15**.

Demon Brother Tobyn comes at you

52

You find a ladder leaning against the side of the house and climb on to the roof. The beans growing on the bushes are ripe. They should have been picked by now. Once again you wonder where everybody has gone. You help yourself to some pods, sit down and pop them open. The beans taste delicious. (Add 3 points to your *STAMINA* score.)

As you sit there munching the beans, you see an Ogre stagger out of the tavern across the way, clutching a giant tankard of ale. He looks up and down the street, takes a glug of ale and then goes back inside. Luckily he didn't see you. To climb down and enter the tavern, turn to **86**. To carry on up to the temple complex, turn to **131**.

53

It pains you to fight your own master, the man you swore to serve, but you have no choice if you want to live and complete your mission. You tell yourself that this isn't him, this is a demon… And it's attacking again.

DEMON BROTHER TOBYN comes at you, snarling, slavering, a horrible blur of teeth and claws…

DEMON BROTHER TOBYN   *SKILL 7*   *STAMINA 7*

If you win, turn to **82**.

54

The track to the well runs eastwards along the top of the cliffs. It is very overgrown and gets worse the further you go. Soon you are hacking your way through thorn bushes and thick vegetation. It is growing dark and you can't see to follow the path any more.

Stumbling around in the dark you lose your footing, and the next thing you know, you are tumbling down the cliff face towards the pass. (Lose 2 *STAMINA* points.) You land in a heap by the side of the road. Turn to **307**.

55

'So you need more money, eh?' says Swann. 'Well, let me tell you a secret. A rich aristocrat called Sir Jordaan Mannly had a big mansion on the south-east side of town. When the demons started to take over Salamonis he told me he'd buried all his money in his front garden under a statue of Hamaskis. He died two days ago and, if I'd been able to get out of my shop, I'd have gone to dig it up. If you want to have a go then take this silver trowel...'

To go treasure hunting, add the Silver Trowel to your Equipment List and turn to **73**. If not, turn to **364**.

56

You take hold of Brother Tobyn's arm, pulling him away

from the demon just as its claws rake down through the air. You get the old man to his feet and run. You can hear the horrible sounds of the poor fishwife being torn to pieces and the cries of the locals as they hurry over to fight the monster amongst the scattered coals.

You run on and see you have two choices. A dark alleyway that looks like it might be a good place to hide, or a wider street, Net Lane, along which a unit of the city guard is approaching. To choose the dark alleyway, turn to **127**. To choose Net Lane, turn to **146**.

57

As you place your apple on the dish, smoke rises from it. For a moment you feel light-headed, but when the smoke clears you see that a passageway has opened up behind the shrine. To enter the passage behind the shrine, turn to **81**. If you don't want to risk it, turn to **406**.

58

You run over to the carriage and open the door to find Lady Webspinn and her maid, Liara, inside, dressed for travel. Liara appears to be comforting her mistress. She has her arms round Lady Webspinn and her face is buried in her neck.

To get in the carriage, turn to **194**. To try your luck on foot and head for the gates, turn to **177**.

59

'I have heard of the Invisible City,' says the Lamassu. 'They say it is to be found on the Plain of Bronze. I have flown over the plain many times but have never seen the city. I fear it doesn't actually exist. If you want to climb on to my back I can fly you there, however, and we could look for it.'

To fly on the Lamassu to the Plain of Bronze, turn to **463**. To ask the Lamassu more about Salamonis, turn to **43**. To thank the Lamassu and continue towards Salamonis on horseback, turn to **240**.

60

You have been defeated. There is a moment of unbearable pain and then nothing. But then you feel your spirit rising free. Everything is misty, hazy and distorted. Perhaps if you can get back to your own body you will have a chance of survival. Your spirit floats towards the gates, which have once again become transparent, and passes through.

You see your body lying where the Obsidian Giants felled it, and you will yourself back into it... You rise shakily to your feet. Turn to **7**.

61

You clamber aboard the carriage and see that Lady Webspinn is travelling with a maidservant, who she introduces as Liara. You are soon on your way, rattling and bouncing down the road.

Lady Webspinn draws her veil aside. She has a kind face, even though she has come from the den of thieves and villains that is Port Blacksand. She asks you innocently where you are going, and what you are planning to do there. Words of warning ring in your head... 'Trust no one from Port Blacksand, and tell no one of your task...'

To tell her the truth, turn to **91**. To tell her that you're just going to visit an aunt in Salamonis, turn to **121**.

62

There's a bang, a roar and a flash of fire, and the next thing you see is a pillar of flame shooting up into the night sky from the centre of the stone circle. In seconds the bier is blazing, and the pall covering the adventurer's body is on fire. All are burnt, the Imps, the adventurer, his equipment...

You will never find the Invisible City now – your adventure is over.

63

The Demon Soldiers smile, showing jagged teeth, and advance towards you. Choose a weapon and fight.

	SKILL	*STAMINA*
First DEMON SOLDIER	8	7
Second DEMON SOLDIER	7	8

If you win, turn to **2**.

64

You give the old beggar 1 Gold Piece and he smiles at you.

'My name is Fazilus Astra,' he says. 'I was once a powerful wizard, but I made the mistake of coming to Port Blacksand, where I discovered I was not as powerful as I thought. Lord Azzur doesn't like any competition in his city. He captured me, and then the one who calls himself Lord Azzur's Eyes struck out my eyes, the one who calls himself Lord Azzur's Ears pierced my eardrums and made me deaf, and finally the one who calls himself Lord Azzur's Mouth cut out my tongue. So now you are wondering, aren't you, how I can hear you and how I can speak to you – but look! My lips don't move. I still have some magic left that Azzur couldn't get to. And, as you have been generous to me, I will be generous to you. Take this. A fine lady gave it to me.'

He hands you a small bottle of perfume. 'It is called "Nostalgia",' he says. 'One whiff of it will instantly take you back to a happier time.' (Add the 'Nostalgia' perfume to your Equipment List.) Then Fazilus offers you something else.

'Poison antidote,' he says, passing you a tin flask. 'My own recipe.'

You tuck it into your backpack (add the poison antidote to your Equipment List) and he grips your hand tightly.

'I see into your heart,' he says, 'and I see that you must follow the Corpse Road, view the magic city from the grey rock known as Mount Meerar and pass through the Gates of Death if you wish to succeed. Oh ... and don't eat too many pies. Now hurry. I've told you all I can.' Turn to **95.**

65

You pull the cork out of the bottle labelled 'Collywobbles' and a cloud of brown gas escapes. The hounds start retching and coughing up green bile, but they're still alive. If this is your first attempt at using a magic potion, turn to **45**. If this is your second attempt, turn to **27**. If this is your third attempt, turn to **419**.

66

That was close, you have survived the poison, but it has still taken a toll on your body.

Lose 2 *STAMINA* points, but if this would take your *STAMINA* score to 0, you are lucky enough to keep 1 *STAMINA* point.

Add the assassin's stiletto to your Weapons List.

To go back to the stable, turn to **401**. To go into the inn, turn to **361**.

67

The north gates appear to be locked shut with heavy bars and chains. You wonder if you might be able to climb out over the walls, but as you step back to get a better look you feel the ground growing soft beneath your feet. You look down. A purple demon portal is opening up. You fall into another dimension. Turn to **355**.

68

If you want to take the Dwarf's weapon to use yourself, add the woodsman's axe to your Weapons List.

There is now nothing stopping you opening the barn door. Turn to **130**.

69

You pull the cork out of the bottle labelled 'Dragon's Breath' and a cloud of noxious green gas escapes. The stink is awful. It weakens the Highwaymen, and two of them are sick in the road, but they're unfortunately still alive. (Deduct 3 *STAMINA* from all of them.)

If the Highwaymen have lost all their *STAMINA*, turn to **262**. If the Highwaymen still have some *STAMINA*, turn to **218**.

70

You urge the horse faster and at last, after many long hours in the saddle, you spot a road ahead. From your knowledge of the geography of Allansia, you think it might take you in the direction of Salamonis, but you can't be sure.

As you get closer to the road you see a familiar black carriage rolling along, pulled by four black horses. To intercept the carriage, turn to **40**. To ignore the carriage and carry on riding, turn to **180**.

71

You choose a weapon and prepare to defend yourself against the Demon Maid.

	SKILL	STAMINA
DEMON MAID	8	9

If you win, turn to **155**.

72

It is dark in the woods. Too dark to see your hand in front of your face. But there, up ahead, a light is twinkling. You head towards it, treading carefully, and as you get nearer you see another glint and another ... and then you hear a growl.

There are spots of light all round you now. They blink.

You hear another growl and, as a cloud moves away from the moon, a shaft of moonlight shines down through the trees, showing you – a pack of TIMBER WOLVES. Huge and hungry. You have no choice but to defend yourself.

	SKILL	STAMINA
First TIMBER WOLF	7	7
Second TIMBER WOLF	8	7
Third TIMBER WOLF	7	8
Fourth TIMBER WOLF	8	8
Fifth TIMBER WOLF	7	7
TIMBER WOLF PACK LEADER	9	8

The Timber Wolves attack you two at a time, with the Wolf Pack Leader only joining in the fight when there is only one other Wolf left.

If you win the battle with the wolves, you decide that whatever was waiting for you in the barn can't be any worse than running into more hungry timber wolves and so you make your way back through the woods to the cottage and then bravely enter the barn. Turn to **93**.

The fight is on

73

'When you get to Titan Square,' says Swann, 'take the South Road and then turn left along the eastern road at the crossroads. Carry straight on down it until you get to Mannly's mansion. Good luck. I'll see you here later ... if you make it back alive...'

You hurry out and go back the way you came to Titan Square. Turn to **149.**

74

The Drunken Ogre squints at you, his eyes unfocused, and takes a swig from his huge tankard of ale. He then bellows, grabs a club, and swings it at you. The fight is on.

DRUNKEN OGRE   *SKILL* 6   *STAMINA 10*

If you win, turn to **99.**

You creep past the soldier's corpse and keep close to Lady Webspinn as she hurries on. Eventually, you come to a long flight of steps that climbs steeply upwards to a door. Lady Webspinn opens the door and blows out her lamp. You follow her through and find that you are in a grand hall with a polished marble floor and a row of pillars down either side. The ceiling is painted with scenes of the gods and the walls are lined with books. As you go deeper into the room you see that there are several men and women chained to the pillars.

Lady Webspinn gasps and runs over to an old woman dressed in fine clothes.

'What has happened here?' she cries. 'I must release you from these chains. Who did this to you?'

'No!' shouts an old man with a long beard that reaches almost to the floor. 'We did this to ourselves. We have observed how a tethered demon cannot break its bounds. If any of us are affected we will not be a danger to anybody else.'

'Thank Hamaskis you've returned,' says the old woman, tears in her eyes. 'Do you bring good news?'

'Alas, I have returned empty-handed,' Lady Webspinn replies. 'Our best hope now lies with this young acolyte.' She nods towards you.

'There was another adventurer here,' says the old man. 'He arrived soon after you left, Lady Webspinn, and we thought he might help us. But we don't know what happened to him and things have only got worse.'

Lady Webspinn touches your arm tenderly. 'You must go,' she says. 'Find the mapmaker, Sandford Swann. Go down the North Road from Titan Square and take the second turning on the left. Swann will help you and get what you need for your quest. I will stay here and look for any books that might help me understand what is happening, and then I will leave Salamonis. I need to get as far away from here as I can. Good luck. Maybe we will meet again.'

But even as she says this there's the clank of armour and you see two DEMON SOLDIERS marching into the hall.

'Run!' shouts Lady Webspinn. 'Save yourself.'

To fight the Demon Soldiers, turn to **63**. To run from them, turn to **51**. To use smoke-oil, turn to **35**.

76

You grab a flask of firewater from your pack, shake it and spray the contents towards the flames. Suddenly there's a flash of lightning and the crack of thunder and it starts to rain – but only inside the stone circle. Water gushes down in a torrent and soon the fire is out.

It's just you and the Imps, now. To try to talk to them, turn to **142**. To attack them, choose a weapon and turn to **33**.

77

You go to grab a harpoon from the nearby stall, but the stallholder whips out a dagger and holds it to your throat.

'You want something, you pay for it,' he snarls. 'Three Gold Pieces for that harpoon.'

If you want to pay him, turn to **166**. If you want to save your money and attack the demon with your bare hands, turn to **205**. If you want to make a run for it instead, turn to **56**.

78

A burst of blue light flashes from the wound all the way up Ulrakaah's leg, surrounding her body in a cage of pale fire. She tilts her face to the roof and wails in agony... And then she starts to shrink – smaller and smaller and smaller – and as she does so, she returns to how she looked before she was banished to this realm.

At last Ulrakaah completely loses her demonic form and is the same size as you, but she still has her two swords, which have shrunk with her. She stalks towards you and you back away until she suddenly stops. She has seen something. You glance over your shoulder. The two of you are reflected in the back of the gates. Ulrakaah runs past you to get a closer look, mesmerized by her reflection.

'I am beautiful again,' she says. 'I am as I was. You have saved me.' She turns and smiles at you, and her smile feels like the warmth of the sun. She is indeed beautiful, the most beautiful woman you have ever seen.

'Come to me so I can thank you properly,' she says. To go to her, turn to **144**. To attack her, turn to **224**.

You go inside the watchtower and climb the spiral staircase to the top where you come out on to a platform with a good view of the surrounding area. Night is approaching but there's still enough light for you to see the pass, running like a great scar through the hills. Immediately below you are the temple and the wooden huts, and four tracks leading away from the settlement. On the cliffs opposite you can see a band of goblin bowmen making camp. You are about to go down when you hear a voice from the shadows by the entrance to the stairway.

'So, you are here at last...'

To ask who – or what – has spoken, turn to **96**. To hurry back down the stairs, turn to **408.**

80

'Thank you, brave adventurer,' says the Lamassu, spreading its bloodied wings out to either side. 'I have flown here from the Mountains of Grief beyond the Plain of Bones. Even my own kind have been infected by this demon plague. I had hoped that the scholars of Salamonis would be able to help us, hoped that maybe in their great library there would be books of ancient wisdom in which I might find a way to fight this curse. But I arrived too late. The city has fallen to the plague. Its streets are unsafe. This whole land is unsafe. All I can offer is to fly you wherever you want... Where would you like to go?'

To ask if the Lamassu knows anything about the Invisible City, turn to **59**. To ask the Lamassu to fly you to Salamonis, turn to **43**. To thank the Lamassu and continue to Salamonis on horseback, turn to **240.**

81

You walk down the passageway and it opens out into a windowless stone-walled cell. A woman is standing waiting for you inside what looks like a shimmering ball of cold blue fire. She is dressed in green robes and it is hard to tell how old she is; one moment she looks like an old woman and the next she looks like a young girl. You have found the High Priestess. Next to her is a bronze water dish on a pedestal. She stirs the water and looks at you.

'So, you have discovered my hiding place,' she says. 'Only one who is pure of heart could do it. I welcome you, young acolyte. My name is Alesstis and I have been guiding you and using my influence to help you make the right decisions. You have arrived just in time and now it is up to you to perform the last act of this terrible drama and save all of Titan. Do you have the smoke-oil with you? I need only one vial. If you have more, you may keep the rest.'

If you have any smoke-oil left, turn to **114**. If you have used it all, turn to **97**.

82

You won the fight, but at what cost? If Brother Tobyn clawed you before the battle, or injured you during the fight, turn to **104**. If you attacked Brother Tobyn before he had a chance to claw you, and you didn't lose a single Attack Round during the fight, regain 1 *LUCK* point and turn to **154**.

83

You are swallowed by the monstrous demon rock-eater. Your adventure is over.

84

You are in the Walkway of Evening, which runs north to south. An archway at the northern end leads to the Pool of Miseries. There is a doorway at the southern end carved with armour and weapons and a smaller door halfway down on the western side. To take the smaller doorway, turn to **101**. To go through the doorway carved with weapons, turn to **129**. To go to the Pool of Miseries, turn to **38**.

85

You pull the cork out of the bottle labelled 'Dragon's Breath' and a cloud of noxious gas escapes. The stink is awful. It's the worst thing you've ever smelt ... and it's the worst thing the hounds have ever smelt. Their oversensitive noses and powerful sense of smell are their downfall. They suck the gas in and all three are suddenly howling and choking. The next thing you know the demon spirits are expelled from their bodies and go screaming up into the sky where they dissolve into the purple clouds.

The dogs are back to normal. They're just three harmless household pooches. They whimper and lick the hands of the man with the chains, who falls to his knees, sobbing.

Turn to **188**.

86

You push through the doors into the tavern. It is gloomy in here after the bright sunlight outside and it takes a few moments for your eyes to adjust. You see a tray of pies on a shelf behind the counter and head over to them. Halfway there, however, the door to the back room opens and a huge, DRUNKEN OGRE barges in. This one has been warped by the taint of Chaos and has three eyes, one on the side of his head where his ear should be. He looks surprised to see you and grunts like a hog. To run away, turn to **131**. To stand and fight, turn to **74**.

87

Everything is growing dark. Your throat is tightening, your guts tying themselves into knots. You know that you will never see the morning, and all because you were greedy... You have faced many dangers, but have been brought down by nothing more dangerous than a harmless Hay Thiever...

Your adventure is over.

88

You continue on down the North Road, searching for any signs of life. Ahead of you, you can see the North Gate of the city. It could be a way out of this deathtrap. To continue on to the North Gate, turn to **67**. To turn round and go back, turn to **108**.

89

Quick as you can, you snatch a vial of smoke-oil from your pack and smash it on the floor. A cloud of swirling yellow gas wraps around the Demon Maid, who screams and falls back on to the seat, clutching her mouth, from which purple steam is escaping. She squeals like a pig and her feet drum against the floor until at last it's over and she lies still, exhausted. When she turns back to normal she looks pale and frightened, and when she sees Lady Webspinn, lying lifeless on the bench, she bursts into tears.

'What have I done?' she wails and before you can stop her, she jumps out of the carriage and runs off. To check on Lady Webspinn, turn to **197**. To leave the carriage and go after the maid, turn to **177**.

90

The Imps scream as the clay pot smashes and fire spills out in all directions. The Demon Gravedigger's long coat catches light and he staggers back and knocks into the funeral bier. He then runs off into the night, leaving a fiery trail behind him. But the next moment there's a great WHOOMPH! and the liquid in the basin is burning fiercely. If you have a flask of firewater, turn to **76**. If not, turn to **62**.

91

'I have heard tales of the Invisible City,' says Lady Webspinn after you've told her your story. 'I do wonder if it actually exists. And, even if it is real, they say that it is impossible to find unless you know where to look. There is a mapmaker in Salamonis who may be able to help you. Take the road north from Titan Square and then the second street on the left. The mapmaker's name is Sandford Swann and he can be trusted.'

You thank her for her kindness and she says something to Liara, who gets out a basket of food and offers you something to eat. To accept the offer of food, turn to **141**. To turn down the offer, turn to **160**.

92

Lady Webspinn lights a candle for you and bids you farewell. You take the right fork, glad not to have to step over the dead soldier. You go as quickly as you dare through the winding passageway until you come to a door. You push it open and step through. Turn to **167**.

93

It's only a horse. And there's a saddle and bridle hanging nearby. Quickly you saddle the beast and lead it out of the barn before jumping on to its back and kicking its flanks until it canters away.

You ride through the woods, leaning forward and clutching tightly to the horse's neck to avoid being hit by any low-hanging branches in the dark. The horse is strong and fast and it's not long before you come to the edge of the woods. It's easier-going in open country, and not so dark, but you're still not sure exactly where you're heading.

The horse wants to go in one direction, along a path it's obviously taken many times before. To give the horse its head and let it go where it wants, turn to **17**. To take the reins and steer it another in another direction, turn to **37**.

94

If you were wearing a pair of swift boots, or even flea boots, you might be able to avoid Ulrakaah's foot as it drops from above, blotting out the light. As it is, you are not quite fast enough to run clear of it, and it crashes down on to you.

You know your adventure is surely over. Turn to **60**.

There are five of them, and they're armed to the teeth!

95

There is a sign beside the road pointing towards Silverton. It looks like someone has been using it for target practice. There are several arrows sticking out of it. To get to Salamonis you will have to go through Silverton, so you set off down the road, glad to be leaving the hateful city of thieves behind you.

You've not gone a hundred paces, however, when a gang of HIGHWAYMEN emerges from some ruined buildings by the side of the road and the brigands quickly surround you. There are five of them, and they're armed to the teeth. In fact, even their teeth are armed: they have sharpened metal plates inside their mouths. Two of them carry short bows, and the rest have swords.

'Thought you could get away without paying the toll, did you?' says their leader, his voice muffled by his metal tooth-plate. 'You look like a scruffy beggar, but I'll bet you've got something of value on you. Oh, we're not completely heartless, though. We'll leave you with the shirt on your back. But we'll have everything else, including your boots. And then, as a show of our appreciation, we'll give you a special gift that will make things a lot simpler for you.'

If you want to give them all your items and weapons and discover what their special gift is, turn to **296**. If you want to put up a fight, turn to **113**. If you want to run away, turn to **309**.

96

A young man moves into the light. He has a shaven head and is wearing the robes of a priest. He bows his head towards you.

'I am Vigo Sabulkar,' he says. 'I came here with a group of followers to try to rebuild the fort and the temple. This has always been a sacred place. There is an ancient corpse road that leads from here to the old burial grounds that once served all of this part of the pass.' He points to one of the tracks, snaking away across a plateau to the northeast. 'There was another here before you,' Vigo goes on. 'An adventurer called Hikaz Mandeera, who went that way. I know that you, like him, are on a mission to save Titan. I saw you coming in a vision sent by the goddess Sindla herself. You must take the corpse road and follow Hikaz, for he knows the secret of the Invisible City and together you might defeat the demon curse that has reached even here.'

To go back down the stairs, turn to **408**. To ask Vigo about the Invisible City, turn to **111**.

97

'If you have come all this way without any smoke-oil...' says the High Priestess, her face showing infinite sadness. 'Then you cannot save Titan. You will have to stay with me here in this cell and pray that another makes their way here who is more fortunate than you...'

Your adventure is over.

98

You manage to get safely back to Sandford Swann's shop and he quickly lets you in while his Man-Orcs guard the door.

'I hope you found the treasure,' he says, rubbing his hands together. 'I should really ask for a cut of it, but I'm feeling kindly towards you. Now, what can I get for you?' Turn to **364.**

99

You have slain the Ogre. You vault over the counter and grab a pie. As you are stuffing your face, you hear grunts and voices from the back room. It sounds like there are more Ogres here. (Regain up to 4 *STAMINA* points.)

To eat another pie, turn to **115.** To leave the tavern and carry on up to the temple complex, turn to **131.**

100

You are outside the city gates. As you walk away from them you feel something tug at the hem of your tunic. You turn, ready to fight, and see that an old beggar squatting in the dirt has grabbed hold of you. He has a filthy bandage wrapped round his face, covering his eyes and ears, and he looks like he hasn't eaten in days.

'Magic has got you this far,' he says. 'But now you have some hard travelling ahead of you. Spare me a Gold Piece and I'll tell you some secrets.'

To give him some of your gold, turn to **64**. To ignore him and walk on, turn to **95**.

101

You are in a small music room, with musical instruments hanging on the walls and a huge demon portal in the middle of the floor. You can see a note propped up on a music stand.

'Castrabel,' it reads. 'As you can see, another portal has opened up in here. I have moved to the small meditation chamber off the Walkway of the Dawn. The one that is the twin of this room. Yours as ever, Fish Face.'

To try to jump over the portal, turn to **342**. To go back out into the Walkway of Evening, turn to **84**.

102

The Demon Gravedigger comes towards you, his shovel raised to strike. You see its sharp edge glinting in the light from the clay pots. Choose a weapon and prepare to fight

DEMON GRAVEDIGGER   *SKILL 6*   *STAMINA 8*

If you win, turn to **142**.

103

'If you want to follow in the adventurer's footsteps I would advise you to get out of town as quickly as possible through the East Gate and head straight for the burial grounds near Broken Goddess Fort in Trolltooth Pass,' says Swann. 'You will need to go carefully, though. Once, long ago, there were walled towns and forts all along the length of the pass to keep it protected, but they've mostly been abandoned and fallen into disrepair. King Salamon has been making efforts to fortify it once again, since it is the main way into this part of Allansia from the south and east. It is still very dangerous, however, the haunt of bandits, highwaymen and goblin raiders, and with every kind of monster lurking in its caves. Make sure that you are equipped to deal with the dangers, or you may not even escape this city.'

To see what equipment Swann can sell you, turn to **20**. Otherwise turn to **123**.

104

As you watch, the demon turns back into poor Brother Tobyn. You have killed the man you swore to serve. A terrible feeling of despair settles over you. You remember how your master's wound caused him to become infected. By morning, will you have become a monster like the old Guardian? You sit against the wall and pray that you will be lucky.

If you are wearing a lucky anchor charm, turn to **154**. If not, *Test your Luck* and, if you're Lucky, turn to **154**. If you're Unlucky, turn to **124**.

105

You have devastated the Demon Horde. While the confused remnants fight amongst themselves, you advance on Ulrakaah, who is furious, squealing at you like a cornered cat.

'I am Ulrakaah, the All-Powerful. No tiny grain of salt like you can hope to defeat me! I have been trapped here for over two hundred years, growing stronger every day, and now it is time for me to return to your world and devour it!'

She walks towards you, her giant feet shaking the ground and rattling stones loose from the roof. Even over the stink of this place and the reek of the Demon Horde, you can smell her, a sickening concoction of rot and filth, and as she shouts, the hot, rank blast of her breath makes your head spin.

'I will turn all upon Titan as ugly and foul as I have become,' she screams. 'But first I will crush you...'

Ulrakaah may be a giant, but she is slow and clumsy. As she lifts one foot to stamp on you, you dart towards her, ready to strike with your khopesh. If you are wearing a pair of magical boots, turn to **189**. If not, turn to **94.**

106

'Ha! You think you can stop me with your pathetic bottles of stinking fairy juice?' snarls the maid, and she looks towards a wooden box on the other seat and then back to her former mistress. 'Lady Webspinn tried her magic tricks on me, and see where it got her.'

Ignoring her taunts, you go to look in your pack, but she slashes at it, knocking it to the floor, and you hear all your precious jars of magic potion smash.

All your potion jars have broken; remove them from your Equipment List. Luckily any vials of smoke-oil you have are unharmed.

To jump out of the carriage, turn to **177**. To stay and fight, turn to **120.**

You only have ten vials of smoke-oil left but this is a matter of life or death. If the creature kills Brother Tobyn, your mission is over. And, perhaps, if you show the locals what you have brought it will make your job easier. You quickly slip your pack off your shoulder and fumble inside for one of the glass vials. You take it out just in time and throw it at the feet of the demon where it shatters, releasing a cloud of yellow gas. The Demon Merchant shrieks, flails its arms and then collapses, purple smoke streaming from its mouth and nose.

'So, what have we here, then?' You turn to see a man dressed in tattered grey robes, a hood shading his face. At least, you think it's a man. You glimpse a pair of red, burning eyes, sharp teeth and reptilian skin under the hood.

'A demon attacked us,' you explain. 'It was going to kill Brother Tobyn.'

Everyone looks down – there's no demon there, only the merchant, blinking in surprise.

'Doesn't look like any demon to me,' says the strange man. And then his bony hand grips your arm. 'You'd better come with me,' he whispers and nods to where a unit of the city guard is hurrying over towards the commotion, dressed all in black, with black chainmail. 'They don't like outsiders here,' the man explains. 'Especially Guardians.'

You notice that the locals are keeping their distance from the red-eyed man, scared of him. There's still time to make a run for it. You spot a dark alleyway on the far side of the market. If you choose to break away from the man and run towards the alleyway, turn to **56**. If you choose to trust the man, turn to **410**.

108

You hurry on until you come to a crossroads. To go north, turn to **88**. To go down the street heading east, turn to **322**. To go down the street heading west, turn to **448**. To head south towards Titan Square, turn to **128**.

109

The crowing of a cock wakes you and you see that the sun is already up. You check that you have all your belongings and quickly make your way to the front of the inn, where you see a familiar black carriage standing ready to depart. A porter from the inn is loading luggage on to the roof.

'This ain't a public coach,' he says when he catches you staring. 'It ain't for the likes of you. This here's Lady Webspinn's carriage. She's a fine lady and she's on her way to Salamonis.'

To make your own way out of town, turn to **159**. If you want to ignore the porter and knock on the carriage door, turn to **139**.

110

You are in a wood-panelled study. There are two ways in and out of the room. The door that leads back to the library and an archway leading to a passage that glows with a faint purple light.

Every surface in the room, including the floor, is piled high with papers, scrolls, maps and books. Eventually, you spot movement behind a huge pile of ledgers. You walk closer and find a creature that looks a little like a man but is made entirely out of wood, sitting at a desk writing in a ledger. He looks up and peers over some wooden-framed spectacles at you, and you see that there are nails and screws holding him together.

'Ah,' he says. 'You must be the acolyte from the Crucible Isles. I have been expecting you. What took you so long?'

To ask the creature who he is, turn to **257**. To go through the library door, turn to **192**. To walk into the purple-lit passageway, turn to **279**.

111

'Before Hikaz came, I thought the Invisible City was just a myth, a fable, but he convinced me it was real and is the source of the plague. He told us that it stands on the Plain of Bronze and that he had found a way to enter it. First, though, he had to find some magical items at the burial grounds, known as Pangara's lenses. Hurry after him. Darkness is falling all over our world.'

Vigo has told you all he can. Turn to **408.**

You hurry into the passageway and Lady Webspinn closes the door just before the demons get to it. For a moment it's pitch dark and you can see nothing, then there's a spark and a flare of flame as Lady Webspinn lights a lamp.

'Come,' she says, moving quickly along the passageway, which twists and turns, sometimes going up, sometimes down, and the further you go the stronger the smell of rotting meat becomes.

'I have to tell you,' says Lady Webspinn. 'I am from Salamonis. I am a scholar at the Halls of Learning here. I travelled to Port Blacksand to look for the wizard Nicodemus, and see if he might know how to combat the plague. But the city was too dangerous and I had to get out before I found him. When I left here, only ten days ago, my city was unaffected, but now... Ugh!' Lady Webspinn suddenly stops.

'Step carefully,' she says.

You see a dead soldier on the floor, showing all the signs of having been attacked by demons.

'This isn't good,' says Lady Webspinn. 'If the demons have got into the Halls of Learning, there may be no hope for Allansia. I thought this would be a safe place. It seems I may have been wrong. There is another passageway here that will take you straight to Titan Square, the heart of Salamonis. Go that way if you wish...'

The passageway forks here. To say goodbye to Lady Webspinn and go to Titan Square, turn to **92**. To carry on with her to the Halls of Learning, turn to **75**.

113

The five Highwaymen advance towards you, chuckling, ready for a fight.

If you've visited Lord Azzur's Palace, turn to **133**. Otherwise, turn to **196**.

114

You give the High Priestess a vial of smoke-oil and she smiles.

'With this as a seed, I can grow as much oil as we need to banish the demons already here in Allansia,' she says. 'But Ulrakaah herself must be stopped or she will simply create more. You will need to arm yourself with both the knowledge and the weapon needed to pass through the Gates of Death and defeat her. To do that, you must first find the Holy Man who is hiding somewhere in this temple.'

'Have a cup of Skullbuster.'

To ask Alesstis about Ulrakaah, turn to **126**. To ask about the Gates of Death, turn to **164**. To ask about the Holy Man, turn to **176**. To go back to the Temple of Throff, turn to **406**.

115

As you reach for another pie, the door crashes open and several angry Drunken Ogres barge in. You're trapped behind the counter and there are too many to fight. As they advance towards you, swinging their war clubs, you realize that you were so close but now your adventure is over.

All for the sake of another pie.

116

There is a rattling and clattering and clunking of several locks being turned and bolts pulled back and then the door opens a crack. You look down to see an angry Dwarf with a thick red beard glaring up at you.

'An acolyte on a quest, are you?' he says. 'Better come in out of the rain.'

You go in and the Dwarf locks the door. The inside of the cottage is cramped but warm and dry. There's a fire in the grate and food and drink laid out on a rough oak table.

'I'm Fossick the lumberjack,' says the Dwarf once he's

secured the door, and he goes over to a table. 'Have a cup of Skullbuster.'

Desperate for any food or drink, you take a sip and immediately regret it. Your head spins, your vision blurs and your belly is filled with fire. You feel like someone is using your skull for a drum and there's a horrible howling, moaning sound ringing in your ears.

You sit at the table and wait for your head to clear. Soon the pain has been replaced by a soft, fuzzy glow and you find yourself telling Fossick your whole story as if he were your oldest and dearest friend. He grows quiet the more you say and busies himself with serving you a fine meal of bread and cheese and mushroom soup. Add 3 *STAMINA* points.

When you have finished telling your story, Fossick stares at you for a long time, tangling and untangling his fingers in his beard. Once again you hear that moaning sound and shake your head. Your guts rumble and then there's a great thump. You wonder if it came from underground or from your belly.

'I have to tell you something,' Fossick says at last, clearing away your bowl. 'My wife, Glossop, died two years back and I've lived here alone with my daughter, Blossom, ever since. She's everything to me. I can't imagine life without her. But she fell ill recently, and when she woke from her fever she was changed. She'd caught the demon plague, you see, and turned into ... one of them...'

There's a bang and a groan from under your feet.

'You hear that?' says Fossick, leaning in closer. 'That's her. I just managed to shut her in the cellar before she bit my head off. I don't know what to do, but perhaps the great goddess Throff sent you here to help me. If you can do something about Blossom I'll reward you richly.'

Fossick nods towards a sturdy wooden chest. 'I've treasure and magic potions in there,' he says. 'Deliver my darling Blossom from her misery and they're yours.'

To offer your help, turn to **135**. To tell Fossick you can't help him, turn to **156**. To fight him for his treasure, turn to **169**.

117

You take a glass vial of smoke-oil out of your pack and smash it at the feet of the Demon Gravedigger. Yellow smoke explodes out of it and envelops the fiend. He howls and writhes as if being burnt alive, while purple steam billows from his mouth and nose. At last he falls to the ground. By the time you go over for a better look, he has turned back into a normal person, albeit a very ugly one with no teeth. He looks up at you and bursts into tears.

'Thank you, thank you,' he says – and then he spots the Imps and runs off screaming.

That's the last you'll see of the Gravedigger. But now, brandishing their knives, the Imps advance towards you. . .

To throw one of the clay pots at the Graveyard Imps, turn to **48**. To attack them with a weapon, turn to **33**. To try to speak to their king, turn to **142.**

118

You walk through the door and realize you have walked into a giant mouth. It seems that Ulrakaah's demons are taking over the temple. Its huge jaws start to close and you watch helplessly as the upper row of teeth comes down. The next thing you know the tongue moves and you are swallowed by its gaping black gullet.

Your only hope is that the mouth won't like the taste of you. *Test your Luck*. If you are Lucky, it will spit you out through the roof. To see where you land, turn to **275**. If you are Unlucky, turn to **83**.

119

You force your horse to wade over to the island and dismount, ready to take on the six Demon Pigs, which you will have to fight two at a time.

	SKILL	STAMINA
First DEMON PIG	6	4
Second DEMON PIG	5	5
Third DEMON PIG	6	4
Fourth DEMON PIG	3	3
Fifth DEMON PIG	4	5
Sixth DEMON PIG	5	4

If you win, turn to **80**.

120

The carriage is soon filled with smoke from the broken bottles, all the colours and smells mingling, and the Demon Maid's laughter turns into coughs and gasps. You are choking as well and your eyes are watering so that you lose sight of her. All you can see is one clawed hand groping in the air. And then you hear a horrible, gurgling scream. The awful mixture has done something to her after all. As the smoke clears you see that she's grown huge and swollen, her bulbous, fattened body filling the carriage, getting bigger and bigger, until she seems to fill the whole space.

'No!' she screams at last and explodes, spattering you with purple gunk.

To look in the box that Liara nodded towards, turn to **140**. To leave the carriage, turn to **177**.

121

Lady Webspinn listens to your story about visiting an aunt without comment and then says something to her girl, Liara, who gets out a basket of food and offers you something to eat. To accept the offer of food, turn to **141**. To turn down the offer, turn to **160**.

122

We built the Gates of Death to protect us all from the demons that were banished to the Realm of the Dead, and only one who is pure of heart and skilled in the ways of magic can pass through without opening them. To open them would bring certain doom, which is why, if anyone so much as touches the iron rings that hold them closed, they will summon the two immortal Obsidian Giants that guard them.

A word of warning. To pass through the gates without opening them requires the ultimate sacrifice. One who would travel to the Realm of the Dead must first be slain by the Obsidian Giants. It is only when the spirit is severed from the body that it can pass over to the other side. But remember, you can carry nothing with you except something that belongs to Ulrakaah herself...

Turn to **409**.

123

You thank Swann for all his help and he lets you out of his shop. As you step out into the street you see that it's blocked by demons who have been waiting for you, hungry for blood.

'Go swiftly! The fate of all Titan is in your hands!' Swann shouts and then slams the door behind you and locks it. If you're wearing the swift silver boots, turn to **162**. If not, turn to **148**.

124

The people of Allansia tell tales of the demon that lives in the dungeons beneath Lord Azzur's palace... Your adventure is over.

125

You enter the hut and find a family is sheltering inside: three children and their mother, who is bent over a table preparing food. For some reason the children appear terrified, and when their mother turns round you realize why. She has been cursed by the demon plague and become a monster. Her dark eyes fix on you as she bares her teeth that are as sharp as knives.

To fight the DEMON MOTHER, turn to **157**. To use smoke-oil on her, turn to **170**. To run out of the hut and abandon the children to their fate, turn to **143**.

126

'Ulrakaah was once a high priestess of this temple,' says Alesstis. 'They say she was the most beautiful woman in all Allansia, but she grew proud and vain. She wanted to use the power of this place to rule not just this city, but all of Titan. She used dark magic to grow stronger and it ate away at her until she became a monster. The priests of Throff finally rose up against her and imprisoned her behind the Gates of Death, where she has remained ever since, growing ever more powerful. Now she is strong enough to create portals and send her demonic forces into this realm. Her creatures are allying themselves with all the twisted forces of Chaos in our world, and when there are enough of them they will storm the temple, open the gates and release their queen. Already there are monsters here in the city. You must slay Ulrakaah. And to do that, you will have to use an enchanted khopesh. There are two, one purple and one black. They are the only weapons powerful enough to defeat her.'

To ask about the enchanted weapons, turn to **145**. To ask about the Gates of Death, turn to **164**. To ask about the Holy Man, turn to **176**. To go back to the Temple of Throff, turn to **406**.

127

'This way,' you hiss, dragging Brother Tobyn into the alley. But you haven't gone ten paces when figures emerge from the gloom of hidden doorways on either side.

'So, what have we here, then?' You spin round to see a skinny wretch wielding an axe, blocking the entrance to the alley. There's no escape.

You see the flash of steel and hear Brother Tobyn cry out in pain as he falls against one wall and then slides down into the gutter.

'Stop!' you shout. 'We're here to save you. We have...' But your words are cut short as two laughing THIEVES throw you to the ground. There are six of them in all.

Your only choice is to fight them... Two at a time!

	SKILL	STAMINA
First THIEF	7	9
Second THIEF	8	7
Third THIEF	9	8
Fourth THIEF	9	6
Fifth THIEF	7	8
Sixth THIEF	8	9

If you win, turn to **187**.

128

You walk on until you come to a crossroads, with streets heading north, south, east and west. To go north, turn to **108**. To go east, turn to **50**. To go west, turn to **28**. To go south towards Titan Square, turn to **149.**

129

You are in a guardroom, though there are no signs of any temple guards. There are three doors here: the door carved with weapons that leads to the Walkway of Evening, a second at the eastern end of the guardroom with a symbol of the moon on it, and another at the eastern end in the same wall as the one leading to the Walkway of Evening, carved to look like a giant book. The walls are decorated with murals of Lunara, goddess of night and the moon. She is shown standing in a moonlit orchard, among trees laden with silver apples. There are racks of spears and swords and golden breastplates near the walls, and a row of double-headed temple-guard axes is laid out on a table. There's a large fireplace with a stack of unlit logs in it. Is it your imagination or is there a faint purple glow coming from the chimney?

To take a weapon, turn to **420**. To go through the door with the moon symbol, turn to **299**. To take the door that looks like a book, turn to **150**. To take the door to the Walkway of Evening, turn to **84.**

130

An animal snorts in the darkness. It has big, yellow teeth and black, staring eyes…

To enter the barn, turn to **93**. To run off as quickly as you can into the woods, turn to **72**.

131

With every step you take, the city appears to grow more solid around you. You hurry up through streets that curve and twist and climb around the rock, every so often crossing bridges built on arches that span the lower levels and look down on the blue-tiled rooftops and gardens that are ingeniously growing everywhere. You pass fountains and pools and channels of water flowing down from the top of the city. Several times, you have to go up a flight of steps or a steep ramp to get to the next level, and halfway up you come to a small terrace built high on the edge of the city. This is where you see your first people, lying dead, showing all the signs of having been attacked by demons. It's a beautiful day and, if it wasn't for the dead bodies and the ever-present sense of danger, you'd stop to admire the view out across the plains, spread out below you in the morning light.

Instead, you press on until at last you come to the

summit, where you find a street of small buildings and two big iron gates opening into a fine garden that looks very peaceful. Peaceful and deserted. On the other side of the garden are wide steps leading up to the Great Temple.

To go through the gates into the Temple Gardens, turn to **275**. To explore the street, turn to **215**.

132

'We must hurry!' Lady Webspinn goes over to the wall plaque, murmurs some words, places her hand on the six-headed arrow symbol on Logaan's chest and presses. There's a click, and a section of the wall slides back to reveal an opening. You can just make out a long, narrow passageway on the other side. It's dark and smells of rotting meat.

To follow Lady Webspinn into the passageway, turn to **112**. To leave her and try your luck on your own, turn to **317**.

133

You have no magic, so you will have to walk the path of the warrior. However, if you don't have any powerful weapons, your path may well be rather short. If you have Lord Azzur's khopesh, equip yourself and turn to **153**. If you don't have it, turn to **175**.

134

You walk to the end of the secret passage and come to a large opening cut into the wall. A row of iron bars stops you from going any further, but you can see through them. You see that you are overlooking a vast cavern. Far below you, several purple portals have opened in the cavern floor, and the purple steam rising from them makes it difficult to see anything clearly. You can just make out glowing crystals in the cave walls, and, on the far side, what look like two gigantic gates. You can't get to the cave from here, so you have to go back. To return to the kitchen, turn to **273**. To crawl through the hole in the passage wall, turn to **398**. To go through the small doorway, turn to **118**.

135

'You're a good friend,' says Fossick, giving you a big hug, and he goes over to push the heavy treasure chest to one side. You see that it had been sitting on a trapdoor set into the floor. Fossick unlocks the trapdoor, swings it up, and then lowers a lamp into the darkness on a string. You can hear horrible grunts and moans and can just see something moving about down there. Could it really be his daughter?

'You'll have to jump,' says Fossick. 'I can't risk the ladder in case she gets out… Just remember, fix my Blossom and you'll be well looked after.'

To jump down into the cellar, turn to **293**. To change your mind about helping Fossick, turn to **156**.

136

The door is stronger than it looks. As you hack away at it, you hear the demons coming closer. In the end you have to leave the door and turn to confront the advancing monsters. Turn to **148**.

Figures emerging out of the darkness between the standing stone

You approach the circle and enter it. There are twenty great stones standing upright, each one as tall as four men. In the centre is a wide, rusted iron plate set into the ground, covered with strange runes that you cannot read.

Around the edge of the metal plate sits a ring of clay pots, filled with burning oil. The flames in each pot are a different colour and coloured smoke rises up into the night, creating a haze across the stars. Standing in the middle of the plate is a funeral bier made of dark, lacquered wood. It has four legs with a wheel fixed on to each one. There's a body lying on the bier under a heavy silk pall. At the body's head and feet are the sort of items that an explorer would carry with him, including some goggles, a pair of stout boots and a walking staff.

This must be Hikaz Mandeera, the adventurer you've been seeking. You'll never be able to ask him how to find the Invisible City now, but perhaps there might be some clues among his possessions. You step forward for a closer look and it's then that you notice a deep basin filled with liquid underneath the bier. You kneel down to inspect it. It smells like fire spirit, one of the most flammable liquids in all of Titan. You need to get off the metal plate – even the smallest spark from one of the clay pots could set the fire spirit alight. The body hasn't been placed on the bier ready for burial, but for cremation!

Now you hear a noise and look up to see figures emerging out of the darkness between the standing stones, grunting, wheezing, and clacking their teeth. They're small but there are a lot of them, maybe twenty. And you catch the glint of metal. As they move into the light cast by the clay pots, you see that they are GRAVEYARD IMPS, armed with curved knives.

They're half your height, with fat bellies, big heads, big hands, big feet ... and big teeth. Their skin is yellow and warty, like toads' skin, their eyes small and crafty. They stop in surprise when they see you and one steps forward. He's wearing a crown made of sticks and leaves.

'What are you doing here after dark?' he asks, his voice rasping. 'At night, this is our place. Your people are not allowed. And we have work to do. Run! Run – or join the body on the bier!'

As he says this, he raises his hands and a much larger figure shuffles into the light. You see instantly that it is suffering from the demon curse. It is stooped and walks painfully, drool hanging from its mouth. Its eyes are a predator's eyes, filled with pure, unthinking hatred, and its skin has turned ridged and leathery. It's carrying a shovel and wears a battered top hat, muddy workman's clothing and a long coat. This must once have been a gravedigger. It moans and staggers towards you, raising the shovel.

To use a vial of smoke-oil on the DEMON GRAVEDIGGER, turn to **117**. To attack it with your best weapon, turn to **102**. To throw one of the clay pots at it, turn to **90**.

138

You jump down from the horse, grab a vial of smoke-oil from your pack and hurl it towards the island. It smashes against a rock and a cloud of living smoke emerges. In no time at all, all six pigs have breathed some in, and the next moment they let go of the Lamassu and slump to the ground, twitching and grunting as smoke pours from their eyes, their ears, their nostrils and their mouths. Finally, six ordinary porkers struggle to their feet and look around in a daze. The Lamassu splashes through the water over to where you stand and bows its head. Turn to **80**.

You knock on the carriage door and it slowly opens.

'Ah, it's you again,' says a familiar voice. 'Don't mind old misery-guts, he's only trying to look out for me. Climb aboard.'

Lady Webspinn is sitting there with her maidservant. She smiles at you as you get in and sit down opposite her.

'So, you will ride with me to Salamonis, then?' she says. 'You will be welcome company. My poor Liara is under the weather this morning.'

You thank Lady Webspinn and settle down for the long journey. Lady Webspinn taps on the roof with a fan and the carriage lurches forwards. Liara, the maidservant, is coughing and sneezing and has a nasty red rash on her face. Her mistress gives her some medicine and the girl looks embarrassed.

As the carriage rattles along the road to Salamonis, you look out at the passing countryside. At one point you see a group of villagers chasing a demon across a field. Later on you see a group of demons chasing a farmer across a field.

'The plague is spreading,' says Lady Webspinn, drawing

down her window blind. 'And it looks as if the closer we get to Salamonis the worse it becomes. But, come, let us talk of more pleasant things.'

So it is that the journey passes quickly. You talk all day, while Liara dozes, and by the time you get to Salamonis you are feeling stiff and restless.

You look up at the high city walls as you approach the main gates. They're built from massive blocks of ancient stone and look like they could hold back an army of giants. You pass through them into a small square, with a customs house, an inn and a stable block. The carriage stops and you climb out, glad of the chance to stretch your legs. Turn to **200**.

140

The box is full of magic potions. You take out two jars of 'Pretty as a Picture', one jar of 'Thick as Thieves', one jar of 'Dragon's Breath', and one jar of 'Collywobbles'. (Add them to your Potions list.)

You also find some food in the box, enough for 3 meals, which you add to your Provisions. (When eaten, each meal will restore up to 4 *STAMINA* points.)

You must leave the carriage. Turn to **177.**

141

You gratefully eat some cold chicken, bread and cheese. Add 3 *STAMINA* points and turn to **160**.

142

The King of the Graveyard Imps throws himself at your feet.

'Thank you, O mighty warrior,' he squeaks. 'You have rescued us from the demon that has been haunting our burial grounds. We haven't been able to go about our business tending to the dead for days. Ask us anything you want and we will help you.'

To ask him about the adventurer, turn to **161**. To ask him about the Invisible City, turn to **174**. To go over to the funeral bier, turn to **272**.

143

The goddess Sindla does not look kindly on people who abandon children in danger.

Reduce your *LUCK* score by 3 points and turn to **408**.

144

You walk towards Ulrakaah, glad that this is over, but as you get closer the smile dies on her face and twists into a sneer.

'Just because I'm beautiful it doesn't make me a good person,' she says, and laughs, slashing at you with one of her swords. You weren't ready for this and she manages to wound you. (Lose 2 *STAMINA* points.)

As her second sword strikes, however, you are ready and you parry the blow. Now you must fight. Turn to **224**.

'Ulrakaah herself forged two enchanted blades to help her conquer Allansia,' says the High Priestess. 'One from purple demon steel and the other from black steel she got from the Dark Elves of Tiranduil Kelthas. The blades have magical properties and in their time were the most powerful weapons in Allansia. When Ulrakaah was banished to the demonic realm on the other side of the Gates of Death, the weapons were taken from her. They lost much of their power and were hidden in the Icefinger Mountains. Lord Azzur somehow managed to find one of them, the other was found by an adventurer called Hikaz Mandeera. Hikaz was on his way here, in the hope of using it to defeat Ulrakaah, when he was ambushed in Trolltooth Pass by a freebooter known as Sinna the Sly. Sinna stole the black khopesh. It seems he had a plan to destroy Ulrakaah and loot our treasures, but I do not know what happened to him. If you do not have Lord Azzur's khopesh, you will have to find Sinna and take the black blade from him. There is no other way to defeat Ulrakaah.'

To ask about the Gates of Death, turn to **164**. To ask about the Holy Man, turn to **176**. To go back to the Temple of Throff, turn to **406**.

146

You drag Brother Tobyn into Net Lane and hurry on, hoping that the city guards will ignore you and head towards the trouble in the market. But you're not in luck today.

'Not so fast,' says the Captain of the Guards, blocking your way. He's a huge, beefy man with a thick black beard and a ring through his nose. One of the guards appears to be an Ogre, twice the height of the others – and twice as stupid-looking.

'Where do you think you two are going in such a hurry?' asks the captain as he eyes you up and down. 'A Guardian and his acolyte by the looks of it. We're not keen on your sort here.'

'The curse has come to Blacksand,' gasps Brother Tobyn. 'A merchant was turned into a demon, in the Fish Market. We can help...'

'A demon, you say?' The captain sneers at you both. 'That's Port Blacksand for you! Come on, Lord Azzur will want to talk to you two. Take 'em, my lads.'

If you want to go quietly, turn to **245**. If you want to fight the guards, turn to **271**.

147

You are in a secret passageway with a narrow hole on one side and a small doorway on the other. The walls have been crudely carved out of the rock and there is purple light coming through what looks like a barred window at the eastern end. To investigate the window, turn to **134**. To crawl through the hole, turn to **398**. To go through the small doorway, turn to **118**. To return to the kitchen, turn to **273**.

148

The whole street is filled with demons. It would be madness to try to fight your way through them, and you look for a way to escape. You see the burnt-out jeweller's shop you passed earlier and run towards it, once again catching a glimpse of something gold glinting in the darkness inside. Turn to **411**.

149

You are in Titan Square. To go down the East Road, turn to **395**. To go down the South Road, turn to **181**. To go down the North Road, turn to **128.**

150

As you move towards the door, a gout of purple smoke erupts from the fireplace and a creature starts to emerge. You can't see it clearly yet, but it's nearly as tall as the room. It lumbers to the table of axes in a cloud of smoke, blocking the way to the two doors at the eastern end of the room. It picks up an axe. And then another … and another … and another.

The smoke clears and you see the creature clearly. Even though it has no head, it is twice your height, with four arms, two facing forwards and two facing backwards, and in each hand it holds an axe. It is standing with what, in a normal creature, would be its back towards you, and where its buttocks should be are two faces, one male and one female. They are both grinning.

To fight the creature, turn to **391**. To throw a bottle of smoke-oil at its feet, turn to **371**. To escape through the door that leads to the Walkway of Evening, turn to **84.**

151

You hear a demon howl in the road behind you and race down the steps three at a time. At the bottom is a small courtyard. On the wall ahead of you is a bronze plaque depicting the trickster god, Logaan, in the form of a crazed clown, with a six-pointed star symbol on his chest.

To your left is another row of steps leading down. Several demons are climbing them towards you. These were once the civilized citizens of Salamonis. They're well-dressed. You can see bankers, bakers, butchers, builders, merchants, washerwomen, fine ladies ... or at least that's what they were before the plague came to town and changed them. Now they have the wrinkled, leathery skin and the dark eyes of demonkind that you've come to know so well.

If you are wearing a silver ring, turn to **132**. Otherwise, turn to **317**.

152

You decide to let the gods choose one for you. You close your eyes, spin around and then walk forwards until your fingertips touch a row of books. You pick one out at random and look at it – *Hither Chaos Angel Died*.

Record the book on your Equipment List and turn to **192**.

153

You carry a very powerful weapon, and, as you pull Lord Azzur's khopesh out from under your cloak, purple light shines out from it and the expressions on the faces of the Highwaymen change very quickly.

'Now, wait a minute,' says the captain. 'We didn't know you had a magic meat cleaver on you. Let's talk about this...'

It's too late for talk. You attack the Highwaymen. Turn to **175.**

154

Outside, a cock crows once, twice ... and then someone shoots it with a crossbow. You've made it alive to the morning and avoided becoming a demon like your poor master. Brother Tobyn's body lies where it fell, cold and still and grey. You wonder what will become of you now. Will you be left here to rot?

As if someone has heard your thoughts, there's a rattle of keys at the door and it swings open to reveal the dungeon-master and the Captain of the Guards with his men.

'Rise and shine, my little sunbeam,' says the captain. 'Seems you're in luck. There's someone wants to talk to you. Come on – shake a leg.'

The guards escort you up winding stairs and along dank walkways until you come out of a side passage into a large, windowless antechamber. Its walls and floor are covered with polished black tiles, and there's a black marble slab in the middle, but otherwise the room is bare.

Presently, two figures enter, dressed from head to foot in black robes lined with fur and their faces hidden by cowls. One of them steps forward. Its black robes merge into the blackness of the room, and all you can see in the shadows of its cowl is a mouth, which seems to hover in the gloom. And it's no ordinary mouth. It is unnaturally large, taking up most of the creature's head. The skin around the lips is cracked and glowing threads of light weave through it like liquid fire.

'Kneel before me and listen to what I have to say,' says the creature, and the captain forces you to your knees.

'I am Lord Azzur's Mouth,' the creature goes on. 'What I say to you comes from him. What you say to me, you say to him.'

'And I am his eyes,' says the second figure. In the darkness of its cowl you see several eyes, blinking separately, as if they belong to several different creatures.

'And I am his ears,' says a voice from above. You look up to see a huge bat-like creature hanging from the ceiling.

'Lord Azzur knows why you are here,' says the Mouth. 'He knows the purpose of the smoke-oil you brought with you. And he wishes to make you an offer...'

A Troll enters, carrying your backpack and an object wrapped in leather. When he sees you he grunts and takes the smoke-oil out of the pack, placing it carefully on the marble slab.

'Lord Azzur has plans for Allansia,' the Mouth continues. 'And the demon plague makes his planning difficult. A powerful sorcerer has sent this pestilence into our world, and every day, as it spreads, this sorcerer grows stronger. But there is only room for one powerful being in Allansia. Lord Azzur wishes you to find this sorcerer and destroy them. He understands that you will have to travel to the Temple of Throff in the Invisible City, and there you will face a challenge that only one who is pure of heart can win.' The Mouth pauses and lets out a dark chuckle. 'So, sadly, neither Lord Azzur nor any of his minions can go there. He tried sending one of his men before, and it seems he failed... He wishes you better luck on your mission.'

You thank the Mouth and reach for the smoke-oil, but the Troll gives you a foul look and shoves you away.

'Lord Azzur wishes to keep the smoke-oil for himself,' says the Mouth. 'It will be of great use to him. But he will allow you to take one vial to give to the Priestess at the Temple...'

The Troll picks up one vial and puts it into your pack, which he then hands to you. With only a single vial, your mission will be extremely difficult. Hopeless, even. But at least you have your pack and everything else that was in it.

'We can tell you only this,' says the Mouth. 'The Invisible City you seek is situated somewhere in the Plain of Bronze. Travel past Silverton and on to Salamonis, where you can ask the learned scholars there for more information.'

'You will need eyes to find the city,' says the second creature. 'Something to help you see clearer.'

'And you will need ears,' says the bat-like thing. 'Listen well to everything you are told along the way and make note of it.'

'Don't worry, though,' says the Mouth. 'Lord Azzur will

not send you off empty-handed. He wishes you to take this with you...'

He nods to the Troll, who lays the leather-wrapped object on the black stone slab. To demand to speak to Lord Azzur in person, turn to **179**. To fight the Troll for the other vials of smoke-oil, turn to **199**. To accept the offer and take the leather-wrapped object, turn to **249**.

155

The Demon Maid falls, mortally wounded, to the floor of the carriage. You have killed her and can't bear to watch what happens next. So, before she turns back into her human form, you gently pick her up, carry her outside and put her on the ground next to the fallen driver. The army of demonic citizens is now surrounding the carriage. Turn to **177**.

156

Fossick grows red in the face and shouts at you, his breath reeking of Skullbuster.

'I fed you and gave you shelter and offered you my hospitality,' he rants. 'And this is how you repay me.' He throws a chair at you. 'Get out! Get out! Get out of my house!'

To fight him, turn to **169**. To run away, turn to **182**.

It has a human face with a plaited black beard and two great wing

157

As the three children run screaming from the hut, the Demon Mother picks up a meat cleaver from the table and advances towards you. You choose your own weapon and get ready to do battle.

DEMON MOTHER   *SKILL 7*   *STAMINA 7*

If you win, turn to **185**.

158

The bull kicks and stamps at the pigs, turning in wild circles, and now you see that it isn't a bull at all. It has a human face with a plaited black beard and two great wings. It must be a Lamassu, a legendary creature thought to dwell in the remote south-east of Allansia. Three pigs are hanging off its wings, their horrible yellow teeth gripping them tightly and preventing the poor beast from flying. It catches sight of you and shouts for help.

'Save me from these monstrous swine and I will do anything you ask!' it bellows.

To use smoke-oil, if you have any, turn to **138**. To attack the six DEMON PIGS, turn to **119**.

159

159

You make your way down the herders' track. It is raining heavily and you are soon soaked to the skin. As you trudge on, you grow more and more tired and hungrier and hungrier. (Lose 1 *STAMINA* point, unless you have only 1 point left, in which case your *STAMINA* score remains at 1.)

The track takes you into some woods, and with the thick branches overhead and the sky heavy with clouds, it gets so dark that before long you are stumbling around with no sense of direction. At last, though, you see a light in the distance and head towards it.

You come to a clearing in the woods where a low woodman's cottage stands. It has log walls and wooden shingles on the roof. A dim light shows in one window. Cautiously, you search the surrounding area. You find a small barn and a woodshed full of split logs and old sacks. You go over to the barn and find it locked. Listening at the door, you can hear an animal inside. A horse, maybe?

Now you hear another animal, a wolf, howling somewhere off among the trees. It's too dark and dangerous to risk wandering around out here any longer. You need somewhere safe to sleep.

You creep up to the cottage and are about to peer in

through the window when you hear a gruff voice from inside. 'I know you're out there,' it shouts. 'I'll warn you, I've an axe and a foul temper and I've drunk half a jug of Skullbuster.'

To knock on the door and tell the owner of the voice who you are, turn to **116**. To sneak off and try to sleep in the woodshed, turn to **203**. To try the barn, turn to **184**.

160

You close your eyes and settle down in the soft, cushioned seat. Soon the rocking and rolling of the carriage has lulled you into a deep sleep. (Add 2 *STAMINA* points.)

When you awake it's dark and the carriage has stopped. You come alert quickly. Is there something wrong?

'We have arrived in Silverton,' Lady Webspinn explains. 'I am spending the night here and carrying on to Salamonis in the morning. If you would like to ride with me again, meet me back here at daybreak.'

You thank her and step out of the carriage to find that you are outside an inn called The Old Toad. So this must be Silverton.

As Lady Webspinn and her maidservant go inside, you take a look around. Turn to **254**.

161

'His name was Hikaz Mandeera,' says the King of the Imps. 'He had come from the Icefinger Mountains to look for our funeral bier, but on the way here he was ambushed in Trolltooth Pass by a bandit called Sinna the Sly, who stole his sword and wounded him. When Hikaz got here he tried to protect us from the Demon Gravedigger...' He points to the funeral bier. 'And that's what happened to him. It is now our duty to burn his body and send him on his last adventure.'

To ask the King of the Imps about the Invisible City, turn to **174**. To go over to the funeral bier, turn to **272**.

162

There would be no point in trying to fight so many demons, but you are wearing the swift silver boots, so you have the chance to outrun them.

You charge at them, amazed that each step you take is five times the length of a normal pace. You easily get past the first rank of demons, and are going so fast you plough through another bunch, knocking them out of your way like skittles.

Now you are past them and racing on – turn to **108.**

163

You follow the tunnel as it twists and turns, going ever downwards. You can hear a dreary, moaning sound, like wind forcing its way through a crack, or the howling of a wounded dog.

At last you come to the end of the tunnel where you find a bronze-coloured jewel glinting in the dirt and pick it up. (Add the jewel to your Equipment List.)

You carry on as the tunnel emerges into a vast underground cavern. To your left you can see a monumental entranceway, now blocked with fallen rocks and boulders. To the right, the cavern grows even larger. There are several demon portals in the floor here with purple gas rising from them, making it hard to see very much. You look up to see two tiny windows, high up in the cavern wall.

You push through the curtain of purple steam and find you have reached your destination at last. There before you stand the legendary Gates of Death. They are jet black and so tall that you have to tilt your head back to see the top of them where they disappear into purple clouds of gas near the roof of the cavern.

As you step closer you see that the Gates are covered with black carvings and figures in relief – the figures of dead people. You can make out the shapes of countless skeletons and corpses in various stages of decay, showing the wounds of how they died. They have been carved in such a way that it looks as if they're trapped inside the solid body of the gates trying to force their way out. Skulls leer at you, hands reach out towards you.

As you get nearer still you see that these are not carvings at all. The figures are moving slightly. They are the actual bodies of dead people embedded in the gates. The eyes of the corpses really are looking at you, their hands really are reaching out to you, but they're held within the gates, like flies trapped in honey. They are packed in so tightly that they must be what the gates are actually made of. And now you realize that the eerie sound you can hear is these poor souls moaning.

There are two iron rings hanging from the gates, one on each side. You realize they must be handles. Can it really be so simple? Do you only have to turn the rings to open the gates and confront whatever lies on the other side?

Now you notice that all over the ground near the gates are armoured skeletons, with bits of them hacked off. There is also another body that looks like it has been more recently killed. This one is different from the bodies trapped in the Gates. They look like warriors who have tried to fight something down here. But what? And now you find a body that looks like it might have been killed yesterday.

To explore the cavern, turn to **7**. To try the rings, turn to **356**. To investigate the fresh body, turn to **193**. To leave the cavern and go back up to the refectory, turn to **460**.

'Many, many years ago,' says the High Priestess, 'these plains were a rich and fertile land, and this was a beautiful place. It was called the Gleaming City, and was famous for its copper-clad towers. But then the War of the Wizards broke out and tipped all of Allansia into chaos and turmoil, and, when all eyes were looking elsewhere, a demon portal appeared on the plains nearby. A demonic horde poured through the portal from their realm and the people of the Gleaming City tried to defend themselves but the demons were too many and too strong. In the end, the city mages used a great and terrible weapon against the invaders. First they built an enchanted prison in the caves beneath the city and once they'd finished it they summoned up a magical firestorm that rained down on the demon army. In the process the people of the Gleaming City destroyed not only the demons but also themselves, and their fine city. All was melted or blasted into rubble and everything that lived, people and demons alike, was hurled into the prison and sealed behind the Gates of Death. It was the only way to prevent the demons from rampaging across the rest of Titan. The once great city was turned into a blasted spire of rock and bronze. A few people survived, however, by sheltering in the caverns beneath the rock and from the wreckage of the old they started to build a new city - this city - with the sole aim of guarding the Gates. They made the city invisible with magic spells, so that anyone who looks upon it believes that they cannot see it.'

Alesstis pauses and looks at you with tenderness. 'You will have to learn how to pass through the Gates and confront Ulrakaah. Seek the one who calls himself the Holy Man. He will help.'

To ask about Ulrakaah, turn to **126**. To ask about The Holy Man, turn to **176**. To go back to the Temple of Throff, turn to **406**.

165

The mouldy cheese is sitting on a metal dish. There are maggots crawling all over it, but at least they'll add some protein to your diet. As you lift the dish, however, you see that it's attached to a steel rod that goes into the wall. It's some kind of lever. There's a click and a section of the wall slides back. You have found a secret opening.

To go through the opening, turn to **147**. To try some other food, turn to **234**. To return to the refectory, turn to **460**.

166

Desperately, you pay the man 3 Gold Pieces.

'I'm no crook,' he says. 'Just trying to make a living. Take a couple of small items as well, if you like.'

You snatch up some items at random before grabbing the harpoon. Add a fishhook, a brass compass and a jar of healing ointment to the Equipment box on your Adventure Sheet. You also put a lucky anchor charm around your neck. Finally, add a harpoon to your Weapons List. You are ready. Turn to **205.**

167

You find yourself in Titan Square. In the centre, surrounded by tall palm trees, stands the statue of Titan that gives the square its name. Titan is foremost amongst all the gods and the statue is gigantic, towering over the grand and imposing buildings that line the square.

You see a temple, three ducal palaces, the great bank of Salamonis and the famous Halls of Learning, which once stood for knowledge and civilization, but which could now very well be overrun with demons. Set back from the square on the south side is the royal palace of King Salamon.

You entered the city by the West Gate and have been along the West Road. There are three other roads leading off the square. Turn to **149.**

168

If you are to stand any hope of getting to Ulrakaah, you must first stop the army from attacking you, and the only way to do that will be by using magic. You realize that the seeds you swallowed have given you the powers of a great sorcerer in this realm, and the khopesh in your hand feels as if it is filled with a demonic energy. Turn to **213.**

169

FOSSICK, the drunken Dwarf, sees that you are itching for a fight.

'A fine guest you are!' he hisses. 'I'm never opening my door to a stranger again. But if it's a fight you want, I'll give you one. I'm mad as hell and twice as nasty.'

So saying, he grabs his woodsman's axe from a rack by the door.

'I'll warn you,' he grunts, getting ready to swing the axe. 'That treasure chest is sealed with magic. Only I know how to open it...'

Choose a weapon from your list and prepare to fight. If you have no weapons then you will have to use your bare hands and are very foolish indeed to have picked a fight with an angry, drunken Dwarf.

FOSSICK   *SKILL 8*   *STAMINA 9*

If you win, turn to **405**.

170

You hurl a vial of smoke-oil at the Demon Mother and

it smashes against her cleaver, enveloping her in yellow gas. She screams, flailing with her cleaver as she slowly collapses to her knees. When the cloud of gas clears, she lifts her face towards you and you see it returning to its human form.

'Thank you,' she says as her children rush to throw their arms around her. 'You must be the one that Brother Vigo told us about. Let me give you some food.'

She ladles out a bowl of stew and you sit at the table. While you eat, she tells you more about Hikaz Mandeera, the adventurer whose footsteps you are following. (Restore up to 4 *STAMINA* points.)

'He wanted to find Pangara's funeral bier in the burial grounds at the end of the corpse road,' she says. 'It's a platform for laying out the dead before burial, but he also believed that it worked as a means of magical transport and could take him to any place of the dead... Let me also tell you what I told Hikaz, which was told to me by the goddess in a dream – "Follow the star". What it means, I don't know.'

Before you leave, she hands you a flask of firewater. Add this to your Equipment List and turn to **408**.

171

As you and Lady Webspinn walk down the wide West Road, you hear a noise and look to your right to see a group of demons lurking in an alleyway.

'It's not safe to be out in the open,' says Lady Webspinn. 'Take this, it will protect you.'

She hands you a silver ring with an image of a six-pointed star on it and you slip it on. Instantly you feel a wave of energy and strength pass through you. (Add 3 *STAMINA* points.)

'I had hoped the plague hadn't got into Salamonis,' says Lady Webspinn. 'Luckily I know a secret passageway that will get us off the streets and take us straight to the Halls of Learning. Follow me.'

Lady Webspinn leads you over to the north side of the road where some steps lead down to a courtyard. To go with her, turn to **151**. To part company and carry on down the West Road, turn to **211**.

172

You go over to the nearest shelf and take a book out. It is very old and bound in worn green leather with lettering inlaid in gold. It has a strange title – *Chaos Angel Died Hither*. You open it but can't read any of the words, which are in a language you don't recognize. You put the book back and take out another. This one is smaller and bound in black leather. It's called *Hither Died Chaos Angel*. This, too, is written in an unfamiliar language. You put it back and look at a third book – *Angel Died Chaos Hither*. You look at a fourth and a fifth and a sixth… They are all variations of the same four words. As you search among the shelves, you realize that every single book in the library is the same.

To choose one at random, turn to **152**. To go through the scroll door, turn to **110**. To go through the book door that leads to the guardroom, turn to **129**.

173

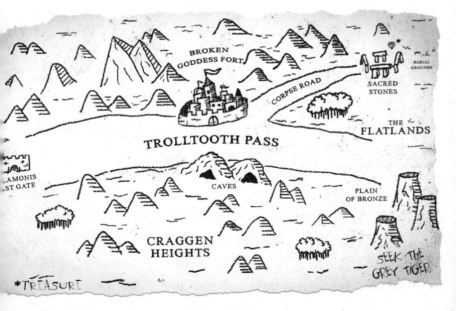

174

'We don't know anything about the Invisible City,' says the King of the Imps, 'except what the adventurer told us when he was dying from his wounds. He said the city is on the Plain of Bronze, and if you stand in the right place and have the right magic items you will be able to see it. And then, once you see the city, you can enter it. The last item he needed was our funeral bier.'

To ask the King of the Imps about the adventurer, turn to **161**. To go over to the funeral bier, turn to **272**.

175

The five Highwaymen move in for the kill. You will have to fight them one by one.

	SKILL	STAMINA
LEAD HIGHWAYMAN	8	8
SECOND HIGHWAYMAN	6	6
BOWMAN	7	6
SECOND BOWMAN	8	6
LAST HIGHWAYMAN	7	7

If you win, turn to **262**.

176

'When I knew the Invisible City was under attack,' says the High Priestess, 'I sent to Kaynlesh-Ma for the Holy Man, who knows Ulrakaah's weaknesses. But before he got here things became so perilous that I had to protect my people and so transported them into another dimension. I then hid myself here so that I could watch over the temple. I can see outside events reflected in the surface of this enchanted water.' She nods to the bronze bowl. 'So I know the Holy Man is here, but, like me, he is also hiding, behind a secret door in the temple kitchens. To find it you must lift a certain metal dish attached to a lever.'

To ask about Ulrakaah, turn to **126**. To ask about the enchanted weapons, turn to **145**. To ask about the Gates of Death, turn to **164**. To go back to the Temple of Throff, turn to **406**.

177

You quickly climb up into the driver's seat out of immediate danger, but as you look at the four black horses you see that they have become possessed as well, with mad, demonic eyes and teeth like alligators.'

A cry of triumph rises from the Demon Horde. They have you cornered... But then there's a shout as the five soldiers cut a path through them towards the carriage.

'Run!' one of them shouts, holding a space open for you. 'We'll deal with these fiends.'

To jump down and try to run past the demons, turn to **216**. To jump down and fight the Demon Horde alongside the soldiers, turn to **207**. To try to drive the carriage, turn to **248**.

178

The Obsidian Giants crack and then shatter into a thousand pieces of black crystal. You step over them, and, as you walk towards the gates, you hear a noise behind you. You turn to see that the shattered crystal is reforming into the shape of the giants. They will soon be back as they were.

To quickly open the gates, turn to **436**. To return to the refectory, turn to **460**. To investigate the body of the fallen warrior, turn to **193**.

179

'What?' The Mouth grows fiery with anger. 'In person? You wish to speak to Lord Varek Azzur in person? Are you insane? Nobody gets to speak to him in person.'

The cracks in his skin glow fiercely and so do his hands. Before you know what's happening, he hurls two fireballs at you that sparkle and crackle as they fly through the air.

You duck... *Test your Luck*. If you're Unlucky, turn to **328**. If you're Lucky, turn to **270**.

180

You watch the carriage drive on down the road, leaving a trail of dust in its wake. You follow it, but your horse is tired now and its flanks are wet with sweat. There's a river running alongside the road and you lead the horse over to it to drink.

You spot a demon paddling down it with a big grin on its face, using a dead body as a canoe. It's clear that nowhere is safe, not the road, nor the fields, nor the rivers, and indeed, the next thing you see is six demonic pigs attacking a great bull on a small island in the middle of the river. The pigs are making a terrible squealing sound, their skin is as lumpy as the bark of old trees and they have grown vicious tusks. Their dark eyes glint with an evil intelligence. Your horse has finished drinking and is nervous of the other animals.

To ignore the demon pigs and ride on towards Salamonis, turn to **240**. To help the bull, turn to **158**.

181

You walk on until you come to a crossroads. To go east, turn to **298**. To go west, turn to **322**. To go south, turn to **208**. To go north towards Titan Square, turn to **149**.

182

As you run for the door, Fossick picks up a heavy fire iron from a rack near the stove and hurls it at you.

Test your Luck. If you are Lucky, turn to **316**. If you are Unlucky, turn to **337**.

183

'All the books in our library have been protected by magic to keep them from being read by the wrong eyes. Let the gods guide you in choosing the correct one. And, once chosen, you will have to get it translated by the Fish with a Thousand Voices.'

To ask about the Fish, turn to **209**. To ask about the High Priestess, turn to **219**. To ask about the Gates of Death, turn to **250**. To go through the library door, turn to **192**. To walk into the purple-lit corridor, turn to **279**.

184

You look in your pack to see if there's anything that might open the locked barn door. If you have a fishhook and want to try to pick the lock with it, turn to **3**. If you have an axe and want to use it to chop through the door, turn to **22**. If you have a fire iron, and want to use it to smash the lock, turn to **47**. If you have none of these items, you'll have to go and sleep in the woodshed, turn to **203**.

185

You are glad that the children weren't here to see the demon die and turn back into their mother, and you quickly search the hut before they return. You find a flask of firewater, a bag of nuts and a bowl of hot stew. You can take the nuts with you.

Add 1 meal to your Provisions; whenever you eat the nuts they will restore up to 4 *STAMINA* points. The hot stew you must eat now and this also restores up to 4 *STAMINA* points.

Turn to **408**.

186

You pick up some dried fish. To keep it for later, simply add it to your Provisions. (If you want to eat it, add 1 *STAMINA* point.) Now turn to **234.**

187

You check Father Tobyn – he's still just about alive. You help him to his feet and out of the alley. Turn to **146.**

188

'Thank you, thank you,' says the poor man as you give him some water from your flask. 'Here, take this. It's all I have in the world.'

He passes you a pouch and you look inside it to find 2 Gold Pieces, a silver compass, and 1 meal of rice balls that you add to your Provisions.

'You're an acolyte from the Crucible Isles, aren't you?' he says feebly. 'I recognize your clothing. Have you come to save us? There was another like you, passed through here last week, a young adventurer trying to fight the plague. He was on his way to our mapmaker, Sandford Swann. Maybe Swann can help you… Go to his shop, near Titan Square…'

But before you can ask him any more questions, he faints clean away. You move him out of the road, hoping he'll be all right, and then hurry along the street, catching glimpses of demons lurking in the alleyways on either side as you go. You stay on the main road, ready for anything, until at last you see an open area up ahead. You run on even faster. Turn to **167**.

189

The magic boots give you enough speed and power to run clear of Ulrakaah's stamping foot, which crashes down behind you, splitting the ground. You race over to her back foot and spot a hole in her boot where it has rotted away, exposing bluish-grey flesh. You stab your khopesh into it. The blade pierces the skin and you are splashed by a spurt of vile, black blood.

If the blade of your khopesh was washed with 'Pretty as a Picture', turn to **78**. If not, turn to **259**.

190

You have come to a large square chamber with a deep pool of shimmering water in it. This is the famous Pool of Mysteries, one of two magical pools here in the temple. To the north, through an archway, is the Walkway of the Dawn. The Walkway of Day goes the other way, south, towards the main temple.

To drink some water, turn to **202**. To take the Walkway of Day, turn to **406**. To take the Walkway of the Dawn, turn to **214**.

191

You slip the robe on and Nicodemus shouts something in a language you don't understand. For a moment his hut is filled with light. You realize he must be a very powerful figure and wonder how he ended up here underneath the Singing Bridge by the stinking Catfish River.

There's a shift in the air and you feel different but couldn't say exactly how. You leave the hut and are amazed at how everybody in town keeps away from you. Halfway up Bridge Street you catch your reflection in a shop window and see that you have red eyes, sharp teeth and the skin of a lizard. So that explains it.

It takes you no time at all to get to the main gate. As you pass outside the walls, however, there's another shift in the air and your grey robes turn to dust and fall from your shoulders. You shiver, suddenly cold. Clouds are gathering. Nicodemus can't help you now. He was right – you are truly on your own. Turn to **100**.

192

You are in the Great Library of Throff. Bookshelves, accessed by a framework of metal ladders and walkways, rise up and up and up, disappearing into the darkness above your head. Too many books to count. You didn't know there were this many in the world.

As well as the door that looks like a book, which leads to the guardroom, there is a smaller doorway painted to look like a scroll, with writing on it that you cannot understand.

To take a closer look at the books in the library, turn to **172**. To go through the scroll door, turn to **110**. To go through the book door, turn to **129**.

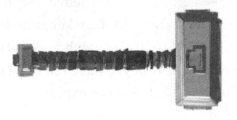

193

You go over to the fallen warrior. He's clad in blue steel and his face is blackened as from a blast of fire. As you search his body for anything that might be useful, he suddenly grabs you with his left hand, and his eyes spring open. He's not dead at all. His grip is weak, however.

He stares into your eyes and starts to speak in a language you do not understand. If you have a Seed of Knowledge, turn to **206**. To leave him and try the rings in the Gates of Death, turn to **356**. To go all the way back to the refectory, turn to **460**.

Her long curved teeth are stained with blood

194

As you climb aboard the carriage, you catch a glimpse through the far window of someone lying dead in the road on the other side. You realize it's the driver, his clothing torn by claws. And now you hear a groan and a chuckle.

'Welcome aboard,' says a deep, gurgling voice. 'I hope you enjoy the ride.'

You turn to see Liara grinning at you. She has become a demon, and her long curved teeth are stained with blood. Lady Webspinn's blood. Her mistress's face is white and her eyes are open wide and unblinking.

The DEMON MAID reaches for you. You are going to have to defend yourself. To fight her, turn to **71**. To use smoke-oil, turn to **89**. To use a magic potion, turn to **106.**

195

The hole is just big enough for you to squeeze into. You climb through it and find yourself in a narrow tunnel that has been crudely hacked out of the rock. You hurry down it as fast as you can go.

If you have a bronze-coloured jewel, turn to **7**. Otherwise, turn to **163.**

196

You have no powerful weapons so will have to walk the path of the wise and use your wits and your magic. The Highwaymen are too well armed for you to consider fighting them yet. You will have to weaken them with magic first. Turn to **218.**

197

There's nothing you can do for poor Lady Webspinn. Liara has killed her. You close her eyes and look around the carriage. There's a wooden box on the opposite seat. To look in the box, turn to **140**. To leave the carriage, turn to **177**.

198

You set off down the track that leads away from the fort. This is an old corpse road, the way that villagers would have carried their dead to the burial grounds. As the night turns darker, you hurry on.

It's a long way on foot. If you are wearing the silver swift boots, turn to **306**. If not, turn to **327**.

199

The Troll looks at you as if you are an idiot, and as he raises a huge war hammer you realize that you probably are.

TROLL	SKILL 9	STAMINA 11

If you reduce the Troll's *STAMINA* to 5 points or fewer, or after seven Attack Rounds (whichever is sooner), turn to **229**.

200

So this is Salamonis. There are many grand houses lining the streets with red-tiled roofs and shady porches, but the whole place seems oddly deserted. You feel a drop of rain on your face and look up to see clouds forming over the city. They don't look at all like normal clouds; they're swirling and purple, and the rain that falls from them is purple too. Soon the road is stained and wet.

'There is a great evil in the world.' You turn to see Lady Webspinn getting down from the black carriage. She stares at you for a moment and then walks over.

'Purple rain means that somewhere close there is a demon portal,' she continues. 'Some powerful being is working its evil. You know the old rhyme? "I want to cause you sorrow, I want to cause you pain, I want to see you drowning, in the purple rain." They say that if you are sucked into a demon portal, you need to chant the words "Exitus, exodus, excitus".'

As she recites the spell, Lady Webspinn shivers and takes your hand.

'I feel terribly alone here,' she says, 'Where is everybody? My maidservant, Liara, is too sick to leave the carriage and I need to find help for her. Will you walk with me and keep me safe? I am going to the Halls of Learning in the hope that the scholars there have found out exactly what is causing this demon plague.'

You look away down the street, which is the main west road into town. The houses on either side have their shutters closed and many of their doors have been boarded up. With its ancient high walls and reputation for learning, you expected Salamonis to feel safe and civilized. Instead it feels cold and threatening.

To accompany Lady Webspinn to the Halls of Learning, turn to **171**. To tell her you are going to forge your own path and bid her farewell before striking out on your own, turn to **211**.

201

You stare at the khopesh for a moment and then drop it over the edge of the pit, watching as it spins end over end, catches fire … and is gone. As it disintegrates, you feel yourself growing weak. Without the power of the blade, you cannot survive here in this realm. You hurry back to the Gates of Death, feeling weaker and fainter with each step. Just as you get there, your new body collapses to the ground and your spirit rises up from it. You look down at the warrior's corpse turning to dust.

You are a wandering spirit again. You float back out through the gates. Turn to **470.**

202

You drink some water from the Pool of Mysteries and feel a deep sense of peace and calm come over you. (Add 1 STAMINA point.)

To take the Walkway of Day, turn to **406.** To take the Walkway of the Dawn, turn to **214.**

203

You make a bed with some of the sacking and settle down for the night. You don't sleep well. It's uncomfortable in the shed and all night long you can hear animals outside, circling the clearing. When day breaks, you are even more hungry and tired than before.

Lose 1 *STAMINA* point, unless it will take your *STAMINA* score below 1.

As you put the sacks back where you got them from, you hear a tinkling sound and look down to see an iron key on the floor. You pick it up and go outside. Sunlight is filtering down through the trees and shining on the barn. You hurry over and try the key. The lock is stiff, but the key eventually turns, and you pull the door open. There's a horse inside, with a saddle and a bridle hanging nearby. It doesn't take you long to get the horse ready and lead it out of the barn.

You jump on to the horse's back and kick its flanks. If you have a book of love poetry, turn to **243**. If not, turn to **223**.

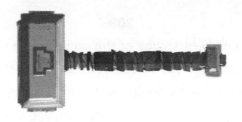

204

You pick up a loaf of bread. It's covered in green mould. You take a bite and it tastes revolting. You are instantly sick all over your shoes. (Lose 1 *STAMINA* point.) You need to get on with your mission and can't risk getting any sicker. Turn to **234.**

205

Prepare to fight the slavering Demon Merchant.

DEMON MERCHANT   *SKILL 8*   *STAMINA 10*

If you win, turn to **225.**

206

You pop a Seed of Knowledge into your mouth and swallow it. Now, magically, you can understand what the warrior is saying and he can understand you.

'I am Sinna the Brave,' he says. 'Although some people call me by another name. I have defeated many enemies in my time, but now I have met my last. Lord Azzur sent me here to defeat Ulrakaah and steal the treasures of the temple. I was warned that only the pure of heart could pass through those gates, but I easily defeated the two Obsidian Giants that guard them. Every time you strike them down, however, they come back to life...' He nods over to where the two giants are reforming and then goes on. 'I know that the Gates must never be opened, but there is a book here somewhere that contains the secret of how to pass safely through. Alas, I never could find it, so I tried to cut through the gates with my enchanted khopesh ... and the gates themselves have killed me with a blast of hellfire... So, it seems, I am not pure of heart after all.' He laughs darkly. 'Not that that is news...'

To ask Sinna about the khopesh, turn to **285**. To ask about the book, turn to **331**. To return to the refectory, turn to **460**. To try the rings in the Gates of Death, turn to **356**.

207

Even with the help of these five brave soldiers, you're not going to be able to fight a whole army of demons. You are quickly overwhelmed and you watch helplessly as the soldiers go down beneath a pile of swarming bodies. Then a pack of demons grabs you and holds you aloft. Laughing crazily, they get ready to dash you to the ground, and you scrabble in your pack for something that might help. If you find a bottle of 'Nostalgia' or a compass, you can try using one of them, turn to **235**. Otherwise, turn to **330**.

208

You have come to the South Gate. There's nobody guarding them and to approach them you must cross a small bridge that spans a street on a lower level. You see that one of the gates is hanging half off its hinges. It seems quiet here; no living creature stirs, and the only movement is a scrap of paper blowing down the middle of the bridge.

Suddenly, you sense movement and turn, ready for anything. It's just a cat, which darts away through the gap in the gates.

To look at the piece of paper, turn to **226**. To go over to the gates, turn to **247**.

209

'The talking fish speaks many languages,' says the Wooden Scribe. 'And, like me, he is trapped here in the temple. I fear it will be hard to find him; the way to his hiding place has been blocked by a demon portal. Perhaps you could jump over it, though; you look fit enough.'

To ask about the High Priestess, turn to **219**. To ask about the Gates of Death, turn to **250**. To go through the library door, turn to **192**. To walk into the purple-lit corridor, turn to **279**.

210

The Obsidian Giants are crunching and creaking towards you. You must prepare yourself for the battle ... and what happens afterwards.

If you have any Seeds of Galana, you may swallow them now, and if you have chosen to use a khopesh you can wash its blade in a magic potion to make it more powerful.

Choose a potion from your list, if you have any, and wash the blade. Then battle the Obsidian Giants one by one.

	SKILL	STAMINA
First OBSIDIAN GIANT	6	12
Second OBSIDIAN GIANT	6	12

If you win, turn to **178**. If you are defeated, turn to **366**.

211

You set off down the West Road and soon see an outside staircase on your right that looks like it might lead up on to a roof.

To climb it, turn to **227**. To carry on walking, turn to **239**.

212

Nicodemus holds out his magical robe, but before you can put it on you hear a cry of pain. Brother Tobyn is bent over, clutching his stomach, his bones cracking. Suddenly he straightens up with a jerk and a snarl and you see that he has rough, warty skin and the same horrible dark eyes, long claws and sharp teeth as the possessed merchant. He leaps at you and is struck down by a beam of light from Nicodemus's outstretched hands.

Brother Tobyn falls to the floor and dissolves in a cloud of purple smoke.

'He would have died anyway,' says Nicodemus. 'Now be quick. Take my robe.'

You look at what is left of poor Brother Tobyn. If you still want to put on the robe, turn to **191**. If you want to attack Nicodemus, turn to **449**.

There in the darkness is a monkey

213

To use the power of the Seed of Treachery, turn to **244**. To use the Seed of Change, turn to **277**. To use the Seed of Destruction, turn to **315**. To use the power given to you by the Seed of Doubt, turn to **382**.

214

You are in the Walkway of the Dawn. At the southern end is the archway leading to the Pool of Mysteries, at the northern end is a heavy iron door. Halfway along is a smaller door on the west side, with purple light spilling from underneath it.

To open the smaller door, turn to **228**. To go through the heavy iron door, turn to **295**. To go to the Pool of Mysteries, turn to **190**.

215

The buildings outside the Temple Gardens appear to be stalls set up for the selling of religious artefacts. You see small plaster statues of Throff, various offerings to leave in the temple, candles, bracelets, medallions, prayer beads and necklaces, as well as leather-bound books, and pottery. But the stalls all seem deserted and most of the stock is lying scattered and broken.

You are about to go back to the garden when you hear

a noise. You peer inside one of the stalls. There in the darkness is a monkey. Its teeth look sharp and it is holding what looks like a ceremonial dagger. To approach the monkey, turn to **230**. To carry on into the Temple Gardens turn to **275**.

216

The soldiers step aside and salute you as you run past them towards the gates.

'Lady Webspinn and the scholars sent us here to make sure you got safely out of the city,' they shout. 'Good luck! We'll try to hold these filthy demons back and give you more time.'

You are still wearing the swift silver boots and are running like the wind. You are soon through the gates and on the road to Trolltooth Pass. You haven't gone very far, however, before you find the way ahead blocked by a group of demon farmers, armed with pitchforks, shovels, flails and scythes, too many to fight.

To carry on running and hope your boots will take you past the farmers, turn to **231**. To use smoke-oil, turn to **246**. To leave the road and try to get away from them, turn to **261**.

217

'The book,' Sinna gasps. 'You have it... Perhaps you are true of heart, though I doubted there was anyone in all Allansia who really was. Quickly, turn to page **122**; that is where you will find the answers you seek...'

218

The five thieving Highwaymen have the following attributes:

	SKILL	STAMINA
LEAD HIGHWAYMAN	8	8
SECOND HIGHWAYMAN	6	6
BOWMAN	7	6
SECOND BOWMAN	8	6
LAST HIGHWAYMAN	7	7

Which jar will you choose from your pack to deal with them?

To use smoke-oil, turn to **9**. To use the 'Thick as Thieves', turn to **29**. To use the 'Pretty as a Picture' potion, turn to **49**. To use the 'Dragon's Breath', turn to **69**. To use the 'Collywobbles', turn to **241**. To open a 'Nostalgia' perfume bottle, if you have one, turn to **442**. Or if you are ready to fight them, turn to **175**.

219

'Our High Priestess, who looks after us all, is hiding somewhere here in the temple,' says the Wooden Scribe. 'If you are pure of heart you will find her.'

To ask about the book, turn to **183**. To ask about the Gates of Death, turn to **250**. To go through the library door, turn to **192**. To walk into the purple-lit corridor, turn to **279**.

220

Fossick shows you to a bed tucked away in a back room. You crawl into it and instantly fall asleep. (Regain 2 *STAMINA* points.)

You wake to discover that Fossick and Blossom have made breakfast. You tuck into a fine meal of eggs and bacon. (Restore another 3 *STAMINA* points.)

'I've a horse you can borrow,' says Fossick. 'He's out in the barn. Give him his head and he'll take you as far as Salamonis. He knows the way so well he could do it in his sleep. And he knows his way back, so just set him loose when you're done and he'll come home.'

You go outside with Fossick and his daughter. Fossick unlocks his barn and shows you his horse. It doesn't take long to saddle the beast and you're soon mounted and ready to leave. You wave to Fossick and Blossom, dig your heels into the horse's flanks and canter off. Turn to **243**.

221

You pick out an apple that doesn't look too rotten. To keep it for later, simply add it to your Provisions list. (If you want to eat it, add 1 *STAMINA* point.) But you need to get on with your mission. Time is running out. Turn to **234**.

222

You don't know what most of the potions are, but you do find three bottles you recognize. A 'Pretty as a Picture' potion, a bottle of 'Nostalgia' perfume and a 'Potion of Power'.

If you want to use the 'Potion of Power' now, add 4 *STAMINA* points, otherwise add it to your Equipment List to use later, along with the other bottles.

When you are done, you leave the room. Turn to **129**.

223

As you canter away, you hear a shout behind you and look back to see a very angry Dwarf emerging from the cottage, brandishing an axe. He yells the foulest curses you've ever heard (lose 2 *LUCK* points) but he can't possibly catch you. Turn to **243**.

224

It is your enchanted khopesh against ULRAKAAH'S twin blades...

ULRAKAAH   *SKILL 10*   *STAMINA 10*

If you win, turn to **42**.

225

The Demon Merchant lets out a hideous shriek and falls to the ground where he thrashes around like a fish out of water. At last he rolls over on to his front and lies still in a growing pool of blood.

'So, what have we here, then?' You turn round to see a unit of the city guard approaching, dressed all in black, with black chainmail. One of them appears to be an Ogre, twice the height of the other guards, and twice as stupid looking. The officer in charge is a huge, beefy man with a thick black beard and a ring through his nose.

'It's a demon,' you explain. 'It was going to kill Brother Tobyn.'

'A demon, you say?' The captain rolls the dead body on to its back with the tip of his boot. Everyone around you gasps and an icy chill runs down your spine... The demon has turned back into a merchant. A dead merchant.

'Don't look like no demon to me,' says the captain. 'Lord Azzur will want to talk to you two. Take 'em, my lads!'

The guards confiscate any weapons you may have. (Remove them from your Weapons List.)

If you want to go quietly, turn to **245**. If you want to fight the guards, turn to **271**.

226

You pick up the piece of paper. It's an old poster and you can just make out the words 'Demon Plague. Meeting tonight in the Halls of Learning'. It's too late for meetings and you are about to throw it away when you notice that there is writing on the back. You turn it over and read some words scrawled with charcoal.

Find Sandford Swann. Go to Broken Goddess Fort. Find funeral bier. Use goggles. H.M.

You drop the paper in the road. To go back the way you came, turn to **181**. To head towards the gates, turn to **247**.

227

You are on a roof with a tower at each corner and a good view of Salamonis. To the east a great statue of Titan stands high up on a column overlooking the city. That must be where Titan Square is, at the centre of town. You can see the city walls all around and gates to the north, south, east and west. As you are going back to the stairs, you spot a dead body lying in the shade of a tower. It's a woman and she's clutching a scrap of paper. You study it. Scrawled on it is a purple circle inside which are the words: 'Exitus, exodus, excitus'. A magic spell, maybe?

There is nothing you can do for the woman. You go down to the street and head towards Titan Square. Turn to **239.**

228

You open the smaller door and go through, only to discover that the room you've entered has become one giant demon portal. The floor, the walls, the ceiling... All is glowing purple and there is a noise like wind howling in a tunnel.

You teeter on the brink of the gaping hole in the floor, nearly falling in. You notice a weird fishy smell in here, as if you are under the ocean.

To try to jump over the portal, turn to **238**. To quickly duck back out into the Walkway of the Dawn, turn to **214.**

229

There is a sudden explosion of light and you are thrown violently to the ground. (Lose 2 *STAMINA* points.)

Cautiously, you pick yourself up off the floor. There are too many eyes staring at you from inside a black cowl. A glowing bolt of fire hovers in the air above you.

'If you're quite finished,' says the Mouth, 'shall we continue?'

To fight the Mouth, turn to **270**. To get up and accept Lord Azzur's gift, turn to **249.**

230

You select a weapon and go inside the stall. The monkey shrieks and leaps up on to the window ledge at the rear of the building. It doesn't look so dangerous close-up.

'Who are you?' it asks. 'You don't look like an accursed demon.'

To tell the monkey who you are and why you are here, turn to **242**. To ask the monkey who he is, turn to **256**. To ignore the monkey and go into the Temple Gardens, turn to **275**.

231

You barrel into the demon farmers, fast as the wind.

Test your Luck. If you are Lucky, turn to **329**. If not, turn to **261**.

232

Port Blacksand is too dangerous a place for a young

acolyte and a wounded Guardian to be wandering around unprotected. You hot foot it back to Nicodemus, apologize, and ask for his help. Turn to **212**.

233

Denka lies dead, already dissolving into a puddle of purple goo. Desperately you search the pile of broken glass that was once your precious vials of smoke-oil. Thank Throff you find one that isn't broken and put it in your pack! (Regain 2 *LUCK* points.)

To search the Potions Room, turn to **222**. To return to the guardroom, turn to **129**.

234

To choose an apple, turn to **221**. To pick up some bread, turn to **204**. To choose some dried fish, turn to **186**. To pick up the dish of cheese, turn to **165**. To return to the refectory, turn to **460**.

235

If you are lucky, this item will take you back in time.

Roll two dice. If you roll a total of 2 or a 12 turn to **330**. If you roll a total of 6, 7 or 8, turn to **46**. If you roll a total of 5 or a 9, turn to **103**. If you roll a total of 3, 4, 10 or 11, turn to **466**.

A person with the head of a catfish sitting at a table

236

You fly over the portal and land on solid ground on the far side. You quickly move away from the pulsating purple pit, hurry down some steps and go through a door into another room. The fishy smell is even stronger in here and you find you are standing in water up to your knees. The strangest thing, though, is a person with the head of a catfish sitting at a table.

'Have you come to save me?' says the fish-thing. 'I've been trapped in here by that blasted demon portal outside. My name is Piscis Austrinus, but most call me the Fish with a Thousand Voices. Others just call me Fish Face, but we won't go into that. I speak all known languages... I speak them but I don't always understand them. Hmm. So forgive me if I sometimes seem to babble, dabble, double, apple, trouble. I work here in the temple translating ancient gnomes, sorry, tomes. Yes, tomes. Have you brought me a book from the library?'

If you have a book from the Library of Throff, turn to **269**. Otherwise, turn to **253**.

237

'Ah, yes, the adventurer,' says Fossick. 'A brave young fellow he was, from the Icefinger Mountains in the far north. Went by the name of Hikaz Mandeera. He came through here on his way to Trolltooth Pass, hoping to fight the demon plague. He said he knew how to find the Invisible City. Said he just needed to look for some magic items in some ancient burial grounds near Broken Goddess Fort. He was going to visit the mapmaker in Salamonis, Sandford Swann, to get the exact details. You should visit Swann yourself, if you pass through Salamonis. His shop's just off the North Road. So, what's it to be? Bed, or a nightcap first?'

To go straight to bed, turn to **220**. To have another mug of Skullbuster, turn to **268**.

238

If you are still wearing any magical boots, turn to **236**. Otherwise, turn to **251**.

239

You press on. There's nobody around, and all is quiet. At last you see somebody up ahead, walking towards you with three dogs on chains. As you get nearer, however, you see that there's something wrong with the dogs. They are slavering and straining against the chains, their eyes are dark and their fur is missing in places, showing bald patches covered with red sores. But worst of all are their huge swollen heads and snouts, far too big for their bodies. They have unnaturally large nostrils, gaping wide, big enough for you to fit your fist inside, and they're sniffing you with a noise like bellows.

The man in charge of these hideous dogs looks normal, however. He may be tired and thin and scared, his face grey with dark circles under his eyes, but he's no demon.

You look around. To your right, on the south side of the street, is a house whose door is slightly open. To your left is a row of steps leading downwards.

To go into the house, turn to **252**. To go down the steps, turn to **151**. To talk to the man, turn to **407**.

240

You steer the horse back to the road and gallop off in the direction of Salamonis. It's a long hard ride and the two of you are completely exhausted by the time you arrive, just as the sun is dipping in the sky.

Lose 2 *STAMINA* points and turn to **446**.

241

You pull the cork out of the bottle labelled 'Collywobbles' and a cloud of brown gas escapes. The Highwaymen start burping and farting and clutching their stomachs. They're weakened but still alive. (Deduct 3 *STAMINA* points from all of them.)

If all the Highwaymen have lost all their *STAMINA*, turn to **262**. If they still have some *STAMINA*, turn to **218**.

242

'So you've come to save us all, have you?' says the monkey. 'Thank Throff! It won't be easy, though. There is evil magic at work here and the whole place is full of monsters and demons that have got past our defences. You are not the first to come here trying to help. A freebooter called Sinna the Sly arrived a few days ago. What happened to him I don't know, but things have only got worse since he got here. You will need to explore the whole temple.

Its secrets are concealed. Its servants, like me, are hiding. Even the High Priestess herself. You will need to find her and three others. Search for the Holy Man, the Wooden Scribe and the Fish with a Thousand Voices. And hurry. With every moment the power of the Great Demoness, Ulrakaah, grows stronger. Now, I have said too much, she has eyes and ears everywhere. Go!'

To ask the monkey who exactly he is, turn to **256**. To go into the Temple Gardens, turn to **275**.

243

You ride on through the trees, ducking to avoid low-hanging branches. The horse is strong and fast and it's not long before you come to the edge of the woods. It's faster going in open country, but more exposed, and you spot several demons hunting in the fields.

The horse wants to go in one direction, along a path it's obviously taken many times before. To give the horse its head and let it go where it wants, turn to **4**. To take the reins and steer it in another direction, turn to **70**.

244

You summon magic from deep within your soul and point your khopesh at the advancing Demon Horde. Taking a deep breath, you yell the words 'Seed of Treachery!' and a blast of pure blue fire shoots out from your khopesh.

The blast hits the demons and they stop marching and stand befuddled, staring now at you, now at each other, and now at their queen. Ulrakaah snarls at them and screams, 'What's the matter with you? Fight! Kill the insignificant worm. You are legion and this warrior is only one...'

But instead of fighting you, the army turns on itself. Some demons even rush at Ulrakaah and try to attack her, but she swats them aside with one of her swords as if they were gnats. Soon all the demons are cutting and slashing and biting and clawing and piercing and hacking at each other in a bloody fury.

Reduce the *STAMINA* points of the Demon Horde by half.

To fight the horde, turn to **453**. To try more magic, if you have any, turn to **213**.

245

The guards march you and Brother Tobyn through town. Ahead you can see massive walls looming above the streets, and behind them a heavy, solid building that rises up like some great dark mountain. Two towers pierce the sky, and from the taller of them a standard flaps in the wind, depicting a pirate ship and a dragon. This must be Lord Azzur's standard. You've heard tales of Varek Azzur, the ex-pirate who rules the city – nightmare tales – and you'd hoped to pass through Port Blacksand without having any dealings with him. But now you're being taken to his palace. Turn to **291**.

246

You hurl a vial of smoke-oil at the demon farmers. It smashes, releasing its gas, and half of them fall fuming to the ground. There isn't enough to cure all of them, but in the confusion, as the cured farmers get up and start to fight with the remaining demons, you are able to get away. Turn to **314**.

247

As you cross the bridge you look down to see that the street below is full of demons, reaching up towards you. If you want to turn back, turn to **181**. If you want to try to follow the cat out through the gates, turn to **260**.

The demon horses are tethered, so they're forced to obey you. You take the reins, crack the whip and yell at them to move. The carriage lurches forward and rolls through the crowd of demon citizens, crushing some of them under its wheels. You look back to see Liara, lying still on the ground. You have to hurry on, and there, up ahead, are the gates. Your path is clear. You crack the whip again and the carriage speeds up. Soon you are thundering through the darkness of the gatehouse beneath the city walls and the next moment you are out on to the open road.

A group of demon farmers, armed with pitchforks, shovels, flails and scythes, tries to block your way but you are going too fast for them. You watch them get knocked aside and scattered. Up ahead you see the low hills that mark the entrance to Trolltooth Pass, which will ultimately lead you to the Plain of Bronze.

You shout at the horses to run faster and they do, sweat flying from their flanks, foam frothing at their mouths. The carriage rocks wildly from side to side and you hope that it won't be shaken to pieces.

On and on through the day the demon horses tirelessly gallop, and as night falls they show no signs of slowing down. You are clinging on to the reins for all you are worth, desperate not to be thrown off. Gradually, the hills become more rugged, and you start to see high peaks and crags, until the road is running between steep cliffs. The horses' hooves are striking sparks from stones in the road and their breath is fiery, and when morning comes you see that you are high in the hills. There is no stopping the horses. They thunder on through the next day as the pass begins to slope downwards. You check your map, trying to find where you might be exactly. Surely you must be getting close to Broken Goddess Fort.

At last, you see up ahead a huge statue of the Goddess Sindla standing atop the cliffs on the northern side of the pass. Half of its head and torso are missing along with its right arm. Next to it are some ramparts and a crumbling lookout tower. Below it are the remains of a fort beside the road, tangled with weeds and thorn bushes.

You haul on the reins but the horses won't slow down. If they don't stop you'll be dragged past the fort and on to the plains. You curse the beasts and yank the reins harder. To jump from the carriage, turn to **267**. To stay on and hope for the best, turn to **370**.

249

You carefully unwrap the object on the slab. It's a weapon, half sickle, half sword, made from a strange purple metal, studded with gold and blue jewels. It looks heavy, but when you lift it, it seems to have no weight at all and weird purple light flashes from its blade.

'It is Lord Azzur's khopesh,' the Mouth explains. 'Powerful against all monsters and demons. It will make your journey to the temple that much easier. And if you slay the rival sorcerer lord with it, it will drain his power and pass it back to Lord Azzur. He wishes you well. Just remember, until you reach the safety of Salamonis, trust no one, and tell no one of your task. Now go!'

The cracks in his face shine fiercely and his hands begin to glow. Before you know what's happening, he hurls two bolts of fire at you that sparkle and crackle as they fly through the air. Turn to **270.**

250

'The Gates of Death are buried in a cavern here beneath the temple,' says Ludo. 'This city serves to keep them hidden and protected. The original way to the gates was blocked with rocks, but they say there is a secret tunnel somewhere in the temple. If you want to see the cavern, there is a viewing window at the end of that passageway.'

The Wooden Scribe points to the purple-lit corridor.

'But be careful,' he goes on. 'Ulrakaah's demons have laid traps all through the temple. I dare not go that way any more myself. Do you have any other questions? Only I will have to write down everything we have talked about...'

To ask about the book, turn to **183**. To ask about the High Priestess, turn to **219**. To go through the library door, turn to **192**. To walk into the purple-lit corridor, turn to **279**.

251

You're going to need luck to jump over such a wide gap. *Test your Luck*. If you are Lucky, turn to **236**. If you are Unlucky, turn to **342**.

You run into the house and slam the door shut. You have got away from the demon dogs. There are no lamps burning in here, but there's enough light coming through a half-shuttered window to show you part of the hallway you're hiding in. It appears to be full of piles of clothing heaped against the walls, with more on every step of the staircase leading to the upper floor. You walk towards the back of the building to see if there might be a back way out. As you go, you notice a movement, and one of the piles of clothing rises up. Before you know what's happening, all the clothing has come alive.

It's not discarded clothing at all. You have stumbled into a nest of sleeping demons. Quickly, they surround you, their claws and teeth glinting in the half-light. One of them chuckles and pulls the shutters fully closed, plunging the hallway into complete darkness.

'We will be kind to you,' he says, his voice wet and slithery. 'You will not see your death.'

The demons fall upon you, too many to fight in the dark. You have no idea where the front door is but you run.

Test your Luck. If you are Lucky, turn to **264**. If you are Unlucky, turn to **276**.

253

'If you want nothing more then you should go,' says Piscis. 'There is no time to lose. I am too old to go jumping about, and forgive me if I have said this before, I am very forgetful, but I have a pair of magical Flea Boots if you need them. Wear them and you, at least, should be able to easily get over the portal, even if I can't.'

(If you don't already have a pair of magical boots, put on the Flea Boots and add them to your Equipment List.)

You leave the wet room, climb the steps, leap over the portal without any trouble and go back into the Walkway of the Dawn. Turn to **214**.

254

The buildings are more ornate and better built than the ones in Port Blacksand, which looked like they'd just been piled on top of each other. It feels much safer here. The streets are clean and wide and lit by braziers. There is a tariff board outside the inn. 'Food – 1 Gold Piece. Bed – 1 Gold Piece'. Behind the inn, however, you find that there's a stable filled with mounds of soft, inviting straw. You count your Gold Pieces and weigh up where you might sleep. To stay the night at The Old Toad Inn, turn to **274**. To sleep in the stables, turn to **381**.

255

Denka has dealt you a fatal wound and she stands over you, mewing with delight. With the last of your strength, you search for something that will take you back in time. If you have anything you may use it, but you will lose everything you've collected in the temple.

To use a bottle of Nostalgia or a compass, turn to **363**. If you have neither, turn to **469**.

256

'I am Grecko the Temple Keeper,' says the monkey. 'The High Priestess turned me into a monkey to keep me safe from the demons. They are taking over. Their purple portals are everywhere... Here, have a banana.'

You take the banana and eat it. (Add 2 to your *STAMINA* score).

To carry on to the Temple Gardens, turn to **275**. To tell the monkey who you are, turn to **242**.

'I am Ludo Hyperion,' says the wooden creature

257

'I am Ludo Hyperion,' says the wooden creature. 'Also known as the Wooden Scribe. I am over a thousand years old. I was originally a dryad, a tree creature, but I have been much repaired and much replaced over the years so that there is very little of the original wood left. Alas, I cannot leave my study as it is my job to write down in these ledgers everything that happens. So now I must note down that you have come into the room and I am talking to you, and I am writing about it... Everything, everything, everything. I mustn't miss a single moment. It is never-ending. I shall be writing this account until time stops. But that's enough about me. You have come to ask about the books, I expect. I suppose you know you will never find out to how to enter the Gates of Death and confront Queen Ulrakaah unless you consult the correct book from our library... I'd better just write that down...'

To ask about the book, turn to **183**. To ask about the High Priestess, turn to **219**. To ask about the Gates of Death, turn to **250**. To go through the library door, turn to **192**. To walk into the purple-lit corridor, turn to **279**.

258

Once again you slide your hand into the dark hole. Immediately you feel tentacles wrap around it. The thiever is angry and desperately trying to protect its hoard. You push your hand in harder, trying to get past it, and once again you find something hidden there.

You pull out a potion bottle labelled 'Pretty as a Picture'. (Add the potion to your Adventure Sheet.)

You're sure there's more inside the hole. Will you risk a third attempt?

To go back to the stable, turn to **401**. To go into the inn, turn to **361**. To put your hand back into the hole, turn to **5**.

259

Your khopesh is powerful and heavy with enchantment, it wounds Ulrakaah and she seems to shrivel slightly as blood squirts out of her wounded ankle. You run in to stab her again as she slashes one of her huge swords through the air towards your head.

Test your Luck. If you are Lucky, turn to **292**. If you are Unlucky, turn to **60**.

260

You run to the gates and in your hurry to escape you knock against the one that's hanging loose. There's the sound of breaking metal and it looks as if the gate is going to fall off its hinges and crush you. To jump off the bridge, turn to **330**. To stay on the bridge, turn to **286**.

261

You don't make it past the demon farmers before they overwhelm you. Now they pick you up and carry you back into Salamonis, eager to show off their captive. The demons in the city howl and caper and laugh in triumph as you are dumped next to Lady Webspinn's carriage at the feet of the demon king. You are just able to struggle to your feet and find that the soldiers are fighting a desperate last stand.

To climb up on to the carriage, turn to **177**. To join the soldiers in their fight against the Demon Horde, turn to **207**.

262

The Highwaymen can't threaten you any more. Working quickly, you loot their possessions.

Add the following items to your Equipment List – one jar of healing ointment, one hard sausage – and one sneaky sword to your Weapons List – and then turn to **11.**

263

'The door shaped like a book leads to the Great Library of Throff,' says the bald girl. 'There is a book in the library that can tell you how to pass through the Gates of Death and enter Ulrakaah's realm, but you can't possibly get in there as the way is blocked by a demon. Don't even try. Now, I beg you, give me all your smoke-oil, please. We are running out of time.'

To ask about the High Priestess, turn to **283**. To give her all your smoke-oil, turn to **450**. To return to the guardroom, turn to **129**.

264

You dart forwards in the darkness, hands stretched out in front of you, pushing demons aside as you go, and... Thank Throff! Your fingers close on the doorknob. You twist it, pull the door open and burst out into glorious daylight.

To run down the steps on the opposite side of the road, turn to **151**. To talk to the man with the demon dogs, turn to **407**.

265

You buy a pie (deduct 1 Gold Piece) and, despite finding what looks like a finger in it, you scoff it down. It's surprisingly tasty. Add 3 *STAMINA* points and turn to **232**.

266

The Lamassu circles and swoops down towards the red rock. Above you, the flock of demon birds is moving in for the kill, shrieking and squawking. The Lamassu lands on the rock and, as soon as you have dismounted, it immediately flaps its wings and launches itself off the edge of the summit to take on the flying demons and protect you. You watch as it pulls away, drawing the demon birds after it. Soon you are alone on the rock. Turn to **427.**

267

You leap from the driver's seat and land painfully in a bush. (Lose 1 *STAMINA* point.)

You watch as the carriage careers on until a wheel strikes a rock and sheers off. The carriage tips over and smashes into a hundred pieces against the cliff wall. Still the crazed horses gallop on, and you hear the sound of their hooves disappearing down the road.

You have made it to Broken Goddess Fort. The walls have collapsed in places, and many of the stones have tumbled down from the once solid buildings. To explore the surrounding area, turn to **282.** To go into the fort, turn to **390.**

268

To drink one mug of Skullbuster is reckless, to drink two is insane. Your head spins and spins and spins and then feels like it's spinning right off your shoulders and into space. You collapse to the floor and the last thing you hear is Blossom asking you if you're all right.

No, you are not all right.

Your adventure is over.

269

You pass Piscis your book and he studies it.

'Ah, yes,' he says. '*Hither Chaos Angel Died*. Marvellous book, marvellous, barbarous, bibulous, bibliophile. You found it. Very clever. To protect our library we disguised every book using magic, and gave them all the same title. We hoped it would fool our enemies and stop them from stealing our knowledge. Do you want to know what this book is really called? Hmm. I'll translate it for you...'

Piscis mutters some words over the book and sprinkles some drops of silver liquid on it. When he hands it back to you the title has changed. You see that it is really called *The Book of the Dead*.

'This was written after the traitor Ulrakaah turned against us,' says Piscis. 'It contains much useful knowledge, if you know where to cook, sorry, look. I have used my skills on it and you should be able to easily read it now. But you do not have time to read the whole thing. It's over a thousand pages long...'

To ask Piscis which part of the book you should read, turn to **281**. To leave the wet room, turn to **253**.

270

The bolts strike you and it's as if your body has been blasted into a million pieces. You feel yourself flying out of the palace and over the town. And, the next thing you know, you reform and find yourself outside the city walls. Turn to **100**.

271

You ready yourself to attack the guards, but, with a foul curse, the captain swings his sword at you. You duck just in time and the blade sinks into poor Brother Tobyn, striking him dead. You now have a captain and four angry guards to deal with.

You are no match for the heavily armed and heavily armoured guards. Justice in Port Blacksand may not be fair, but it is swift and brutal.

Before it has really begun, your adventure is over.

272

You walk over to the wooden platform.

'That is Pangara's Funeral Bier,' says the King of the Imps. 'It cannot be harmed by fire and has the power to carry you to any place of the dead... If you know its secrets.'

You look at the cloth covering the body lying on the bier. There are pictures stitched into it. You can see what looks like the image of a city, made to look as if it's glowing with a blue light. Nearby are three mountains, with a man standing on the peak of one wearing what look like goggles. There's a gold thread running from him to the city and above him is what looks like a bronze-coloured star.

'We made the pall ourselves,' says the King, 'and showed everything the adventurer had told us about. He wanted to go to the Invisible City – so now he can. We will burn him, together with all the things he'll need for his journey into the next world.'

You look at the objects. The goggles are made of leather and brass with smoked glass lenses. There's also a rolled-up map, a bronze star about the size of a dinner plate, a pair of stout boots, a walking staff, a drinking canteen and a bronze compass.

To explain your quest to the King of the Imps and ask him if you can take some of the items, turn to **300**. To kill him and simply take all the items, choose a weapon and turn to **287**.

273

You are in the temple kitchens. There's a huge fireplace with grilling racks and hooks for cauldrons. Shelves of pots and pans line the walls and there's a great chopping block in the middle of the room with a meat cleaver embedded in it. At the end opposite the door, there are stacks of crates and baskets filled with food. (If you want to take the cleaver, add it to your Weapons List.)

The food looks like it has been here for some time and most of it is mouldy or rotten. You are hungry, though, and search among it for something to eat. You find some apples, some stale bread, some dried fish and some stinky, rancid cheese on a metal dish, crawling with maggots.

To examine the food more closely, turn to **234.** To return to the refectory, turn to **460.**

274

The inn is warm and the landlord welcoming. If you want to eat, turn to **294.** If you want to go straight to bed, turn to **361.**

275

You are in the Temple Gardens, which are planted with healing herbs and sweet-scented flowers. There's a fishpond in the middle with a fountain depicting Hydana, the God of the Oceans, spouting water from his mouth. You follow a gravel pathway over to a flight of steps leading to the main temple building, its silver dome towering above you. You climb the steps, pass between some pillars and come to a walkway where you see gold letters inlaid into the marble floor – The Aisle Of Guardians. Turn to **288**.

276

You dart forwards in the darkness, hands stretched out in front of you, pushing demons aside as you go, and run straight into a wall. You fall over on to your behind, stunned. Demons close in all around you, sniggering and hissing, and you pray that this will be over quickly.

You realize that this is the future of Allansia, of Titan itself. It will become a world of demons. You have a last chance to save yourself, though. If you have a compass, turn to **289**. If you have a bottle of Nostalgia perfume, turn to **302**. If you have neither of these things...

Your adventure is over.

277

The demons are climbing over each other to get to you in a churning mass of corrupted flesh. You slash your khopesh towards them and shout the words, 'Seed of Change!' A green flame blasts from the tip of the blade and a ripple passes through the horde, changing the demons as it goes. They are transforming back into harmless birds and beasts, some have even changed into fish and are flopping about on the ground, but not all...

Reduce the *STAMINA* points of the Demon Horde by half and reduce their *SKILL* points by half.

To fight the horde, turn to **453**. To try more magic, if you have any, turn to **213.**

278

You slowly slide your hand into the hole – deeper, deeper, deeper ... until you touch something warm... Skin.

You have touched the Hay Thiever. It jerks away from you and you feel its finger-like tentacles probing your hand. It gives you a gummy wet bite, but you ignore it and push the creature aside. And now you feel something else. You were right. The hole is filled with things the creature has taken. The tables are turned now. You are thieving from the Hay Thiever. You manage to get hold of something and pull it out of the hole.

It's a purse. You open it. It's full of money. (Add 5 Gold Pieces to your Adventure Sheet.)

To go back to the stable, turn to **401**. To go into the inn, turn to **361**. To put your hand back into the hole, turn to **258**.

279

You are in a long, narrow passageway, lined with more bookshelves. At one end is the door to the Wooden Scribe's study, at the other is a window through which purple light is entering. More purple light is coming from under a slatted doorway halfway along the passage. Opposite the doorway are some steps leading downwards.

To look through the window, turn to **303**. To go down the steps, turn to **385**. To go through the slatted doorway, turn to **443**. To return to the study, turn to **110**.

280

The Lamassu glides down towards the sandy-coloured rock, but before you can get there the demon birds attack and tear at its wings. You just have time to jump off before the poor creature crashes into the side of the rock column and then falls lifelessly to the bottom, the birds spiralling down after it. You search the top of the rock. There is nothing to see here, nothing to eat or drink ... and no way down. Turn to **437**.

281

'I can translate books, but I rarely read them,' says Piscis. 'I'm afraid I don't know which part of the book will help you. You need to find Sinna the Sly, a freebooter who came here recently. He knew which page you need to read, but could never find the right book. Whereas you have found the book but don't know the page! That would be quite funny if the whole world wasn't about to end.'

Turn to **253**.

282

You go over to the shattered carriage and find poor Lady Webspinn's body where it has been thrown into the road. You bury her beneath some rocks and then remember that she travelled with a basket of food. You search for it and find it under one of the carriage seats. You open the basket and find a meal of ham, some bread and cheese.

To eat a meal, add up to 4 *STAMINA* points. Alternatively, if you want to save it for later, add 1 meal to your Provisions.

To explore the road further, turn to **307**. To go into the fort, turn to **390**.

283

'The High Priestess is hiding somewhere in the temple,' says Denka, her eyes glowing with excitement. 'I know not where, as I am trapped in here. Every time I try to get out, a demon appears from the fireplace in the guardroom and stops me. So I am your only hope. I never thought the High Priestess would turn out to be such a coward. You must quickly give me your smoke-oil. Quickly, quickly, quickly!'

To give Denka all your smoke-oil, turn to **450**. To ask her what's behind the door carved to look like a book, turn to **263**. To return to the guardroom, turn to **129**.

284

Swann rummages around below his counter and lifts up a carved wooden box inlaid with mother-of-pearl. It has a simple-looking lock on it.

'If you want it,' says Swann. 'I can let you have it for 10 Gold Pieces.'

To buy it, pay 10 Gold Pieces and turn to **464**. Otherwise, turn to **364**.

285

'The black khopesh is one of only two weapons that can defeat the Queen of Demons, Ulrakaah, who lurks on the other side of the Gates,' whispers Sinna, his voice growing feeble. 'I thought to kill her and steal her treasures... I had done everything I needed to do. I had even washed my blade in a potion that would return Ulrakaah to her normal beautiful form ... but I couldn't get to her, and now my blade is embedded in the gates. Perhaps, if you could get through them, you could grab the khopesh from the other side and use it. But you will need to find the book first if you want to get that far...'

To ask Sinna about the book, turn to **331**. To return to the refectory, turn to **460**. To try the rings in the Gates of Death, turn to **356**.

286

The gate swings round and crushes you against the wall of the gatehouse.

Your adventure is over.

287

Quick as a flash, you strike the King dead and then turn on the other four imps. Blades clash against blades and sparks fly as they defend themselves. The next thing you know, there's a great WHOOMPH! and the liquid in the basin is burning fiercely. A spark must have ignited it. Turn to **62.**

288

The Aisle of Guardians runs east to west. With the Temple Gardens at the east entrance and the Temple of Throff at the west end. There are statues all along its length, depicting previous priests and priestesses, the oldest ones closest to the gardens. As you walk down the aisle you see an empty pedestal. One of the statues is missing. There are two chambers off the aisle, one on the north side, one on the south. The one on the north side smells of rotting meat.

To explore it further, turn to **301**. The second chamber has a faint purple glow coming from inside it. To explore this south chamber, turn to **319**. To go the main temple, turn to **387**.

289

You fumble for your compass and pull it out of your pocket. As you clutch it tightly you feel it shaking as the pointer spins round and round, and now you feel the whole world spinning with it – the compass is taking you back in time and space.

Turn to **466**.

'Oh, you've chosen well,' says Fossick. 'Some of those items can be used right now if you like. Let me tell you what they do.' And so the Dwarf does just that.

The jewelled warhammer is a powerful weapon against demons. The Deathstone will drain your enemy's *STAMINA* by 5 points, but it will only work three times. The Horn of Plenty will restore your *STAMINA* to its Initial level; you can use it any time, but only once. If you ever lose a fight, the Harp of Healing will restore 8 *STAMINA* points to you, but only once. For as long as you wear the Hero's Medallion it will raise your *SKILL* score by 2 points.

'The medallion was given to me by a young adventurer who passed this way, to pay me for food and a bed,' explains Fossick. 'And talking of beds, you look tired. You should stay the night and rest, but first, why not share another mug of Skullbuster with me, to celebrate?'

To ask about the adventurer, turn to **237**. To go straight to bed, turn to **220**. To have another mug of Skullbuster, turn to **268.**

You and Brother Tobyn walk miserably along Palace Street, a guard on either side of you, the captain in front and the Ogre plodding along behind.

'Azzur don't like outsiders,' says the captain. 'Azzur don't like Guardians. Azzur don't like short people... Azzur don't like anyone.' He laughs. 'What d'you s'pose he'll do with them, Borgor?'

'Boil 'em in Troll's wee,' says the Ogre.

'Make 'em eat their own feet,' says another guard.

'Use their guts to make strings for his musicians and then play a merry jig as he feeds them to his pigs,' says the last guard.

The guards are still chuckling and suggesting ever more horrible punishments when you arrive at the immense iron gates in the wall of Lord Azzur's palace. They creak open and you pass into the shadows on the other side. There are formal gardens here and a carriageway leading to Lord Azzur's palace, but the guards don't take you up the wide stone steps to the main entrance; instead they take you round to a side door and then down a winding staircase lit by flaming torches.

'If I could only speak to Lord Azzur,' says Brother Tobyn. 'We are here to help the people of Allansia. I bring smoke-oil to cure the plague. We are on a mission to reach the High Priestess at the temple of healing...'

'Is that right?' says the captain. 'I'll be sure to tell my master, he'll be absolutely fascinated, but in the meantime you can make yourselves comfortable in here...'

So saying, he takes your backpack and pushes you and Brother Tobyn into a dungeon, before slamming the door shut behind you.

Until you get your pack back, none of the items on your list that you have collected so far are available to you – including the smoke-oil.

You have been put into a large cell. The only light comes in through a barred window in an iron-studded door, creating a small pool around you and Brother Tobyn. In the gloom nearby you can see a pile of human bones and skulls. You can hear scuttling in the darkness, low moans and the drip, drip, drip of water. You take a step outside the circle of light and pause. Part of you wants to explore the rest of the dungeon to see who, or what, you are sharing the space with, but a larger part of you

The demon plague has made her look like some immense, leathery to

tells you to stay with Brother Tobyn and not risk finding out what hides in the darkness.

If you want to explore the cell, turn to **311**. If you want to stay put and protect Brother Tobyn, turn to **332.**

292

You dodge her blow and stab her again with your khopesh, inflicting another wound. You are now drenched in her blood which is thick and sticky and black, and the more she loses, the more she seems to shrivel and shrink. She still has some of her strength left, however, and as you go in for another strike she brings both swords whistling down towards you. *Test your Luck* again. If you are Lucky, turn to **349**. If you are Unlucky, turn to **60.**

293

Steeling yourself, you jump down into the cellar. As you land, something moves in the shadows and there's a hissing, wheezing sound. You grab the lamp and hold it up.

There stands Blossom. She's half your height, but the demon plague has made her look like some immense, leathery toad. Her lips are thick and swollen, her eyes are dark, and claws extend from her fingers and toes. Wild, tangled red hair sticks straight out from her head in all directions. She smiles at you, showing a row of needle-like teeth, and burps. The smell is awful in this cramped space.

It looks like she's been eating a pig. There's a pile of bones at her feet. She picks up its jawbone, the muscles standing out along her powerful-looking arms, and advances slowly, shaking her head from side to side.

To fight BLOSSOM, turn to **334**. To use a vial of smoke-oil, turn to **438**. To try a magic potion, if you have any, turn to **313**. To ask Fossick to pull you up out of here, turn to **357**.

294

You settle down at a table and soon the landlord brings you a bowl of thick broth and some bread. (Deduct 1 Gold Piece and add 3 *STAMINA* points.)

You notice three people sat at the next table. They are keeping themselves to themselves, and have green hoods shading their faces. You look closer. Are they people at all? One turns to you, as if reading your thoughts, and you see that she is a half-elf. You know that many of her kind, who are half human and half elf, live in the Great Forest of Yore, but you still wouldn't expect to see one here in Silverton.

'You're wondering what we're doing here, aren't you?' she says, again seeming to read your thoughts. 'Our kind are affected by this demon plague just as badly as yours. The forests have become unsafe. I recognize your clothes. You're an acolyte from the Crucible Isles, aren't you? Have you come to help us?'

To tell the half-elf of your mission, turn to **340**. If you want to lie and say you are just a weary traveller, turn to **320**.

295

You are in a long hall running roughly east to west, with wooden walls and a high ceiling. It is full of bunk beds. This must be the dormitory where the priests and the acolytes and the temple workers sleep. The walls are covered with paintings of Glantanka, the Sun Goddess, and there are three doors here: the heavy iron door leading to the Walkway of the Dawn, another at the eastern end of the dormitory with a sun symbol on it, and a third in the same wall as the one leading to the Walkway of the Dawn with a symbol of wheat on it.

To go through the door with the sun symbol, turn to **308**. To take the door with the wheat symbol, turn to **460**. To go through the heavy iron door to the Walkway of the Dawn, turn to **214**.

296

True to their word, the five Highwaymen strip you of all your belongings and most of your clothes. They drop the things they don't want in the road and then walk off back to their hideout, chuckling and dividing their loot as they go. Your chances of getting to the Invisible City seem pretty slim now. To add to your misery it starts to rain. You trudge on. Then there's a shout from behind you.

'Hoi!' the gang leader calls out. 'You must think we're a right bunch of rotters. We forgot to give you your special gift. Here you go...'

You watch as one of them notches an arrow to his bow and fires it at you. The arrow hits you in the chest and you fall to the ground. As the light from the sun seems to dim, your hand closes on something lying in the road.

If you have the brass compass, turn to **346**. If you have a bottle of 'Nostalgia', turn to **442**. If you have neither, turn to **421**.

297

The Lamassu alights gently on top of the grey rock. You stay on its back, looking all around, but can see no signs of any city.

'It is not safe here,' says the Lamassu, who is keeping an eye on the circling demon birds. 'You should go back and try to learn more.'

To dismount and let the Lamassu fight the birds, turn to **310**. To take off from the summit and fly back to Salamonis for more information, turn to **323**.

298

Ahead of you, you can see a beautiful mansion with well-kept gardens. There is a statue of Hamaskis, God of Learning, standing on the lawn, holding an open book. You hurry towards the mansion, but when you get there you find the front gate locked. You climb up on to one of the gateposts and then grab the low-hanging branch of a pear tree growing in the garden and climb into it. You are able to get to the statue from the tree and lower yourself down on to it. It begins to teeter, however, and then falls over, spilling you on to the lawn.

If you have a trowel, turn to **318**. If not then turn to **338**.

299

You are in a room full of different coloured potions, jars, oils, powders and liquids, as well as an array of magical and scientific apparatus, including a bronze crucible.

'Welcome to the Potions Room,' says a young, bald girl, dressed in orange temple robes, and she bows to you. 'My name is Denka Mansell. I am apprentice to the High Priestess and help her create all her magic potions here. I know who you are. We have been waiting for you. Have you brought the smoke-oil? Give me all of what you have so I can get to work. The quicker we can make more of it and cure the demon curse, the better. We don't need the High Priestess, she has deserted us and let us all down.'

To ask about the High Priestess, turn to **283**. To give Denka all your smoke-oil, if you still have some, turn to **450**. To ask Denka what's behind the door that looks like a giant book, turn to **263**. To return to the guardroom, turn to **129**.

300

'Hikaz the adventurer must have his belongings with him,' says the King. 'Or he will become lost on the other side. But your quest is the same as his was, and you have rid us of the Demon Gravedigger, so I think he would want you to have something. I can let you take three items and you can borrow the bier itself. I have no idea which items you might need, so it is your choice...'

If you want to simply kill the King and take all the items, choose a weapon and turn to **287**. Otherwise, choose three of the following items – the bier goggles, the map, the bronze star, the boots, the staff, the canteen, the bronze compass – and turn to **312**.

301

Inside the first chamber you find a group of dead temple guards, wearing bronze armour and dark blue cloaks. It looks as if they've been poisoned. Their faces are purple and bloated. Each one clutches a temple guard's axe in his dead hands – no defence against poison. (If you want to add a Temple Guard's Axe to your Weapons List, then do so.)

To explore the south chamber, turn to **319**. To leave the chamber and walk down the aisle to the main temple, turn to **387**.

302

You fumble in your pack for anything that might help you and your fingers close on the bottle of Nostalgia perfume. You pull it out and take out the cork with your teeth. The smell of pears wafts out. You hear a voice say, 'Mmm, nice smell. What is it?' and the next moment you feel yourself being pulled out of time and space. The perfume is taking you back to an earlier point in your adventure. Turn to **466.**

303

You walk up to the window. It is made of very thick glass and sits in an iron frame overlooking a huge cavern. You look down to see several purple portals in the rock floor from which gas is rising and making it hard to see anything else. But you think you can just make out the shapes of two massive gates on the far side. You can't get to the cave from here, so you have to go back. Turn to **279.**

304

'That box has gone for good,' says Swann. Turn to **364.**

305

Ignored by the customers of the pie shop, who are busy stuffing their faces, one of the thieves keeps watch over you and Brother Tobyn while the other hurries off. The smell of the pies is torture, but you know you're not going to get a meal any time soon, and, before you know it, the second thief comes back in. He's brought with him the Captain of the Guard you saw earlier.

'Well, well, well,' says the captain, tossing a coin to the grinning thief. 'What have we here? I think you two had better come with us.'

The thieves remove the magic potion jars from your pack while the guards grab you. One of them appears to be an Ogre, twice the height of the others – and twice as stupid looking.

Remove the potions from your Adventure Sheet and turn to **291**.

306

It takes no time to get to the burial grounds. You see grave markers and mausoleums on either side of the track and then, ahead of you, you see a circle of mighty stones, black against the starry sky. There are coloured lights blazing inside the circle and a pillar of coloured smoke rises up to the heavens. Turn to **137**.

307

You walk a little way along the road and hear a whizzing sound. You look up to see a group of Goblin archers on top of the cliffs on the southern side of the pass, firing arrows down at you. You spot a cave beneath them. To run back to the fort, turn to **321**. To shelter in the cave, turn to **335**.

308

You push open the door with the symbol of the sun on it and walk through into a stone-walled corridor with prayer cells on either side. You walk along, checking each cell. They all appear to be empty, but then, as you step into the last one, you find a hideous creature squatting there. It has no body, only a giant head, with arms and legs sticking out of it. It has five black eyes, a wide mouth with broken teeth and a snout like a pig.

To run back to the dormitory, turn to **295**. To fight the hideous creature, choose a weapon and turn to **368**.

309

You set off running through the tall grass at the side of the road, and then jump over a fence into a cornfield. You hear a whizzing noise and turn to see that one of the Highwaymen has fired an arrow after you.

Test your Luck. If you are Lucky, turn to **396**. If you are Unlucky, turn to **339**.

310

You slip off the Lamassu's back and watch as it takes off and flies up towards the demon birds. A terrible battle ensues and you can do nothing to help as the poor creature spirals down to the ground, mobbed by pecking, scratching birds. You look around the summit. There is nothing to see here on the grey rock, not even a way down. Turn to **437**.

311

Carefully, your heart seemingly stuck in your throat, you venture deeper into the darkness. Shuffling forward, your arms stretched out in front of you, your fingers probe the gloom. Further, further... Nothing. The cell is much bigger than you imagined. You grow bolder and move faster, all the while expecting your fingers to touch cold, damp, stone. And now you hear a voice, whispering in the darkness.

'Come here. I want to help you...'

If you want to go towards the voice, turn to **352**. If you want to hurry back to Brother Tobyn, turn to **332**.

312

If you have chosen the boots, you discover that they are bronze-clad swift boots. If you don't already have a pair of swift boots, put them on. If you chose the canteen, whenever you want to drink from it, add 3 *STAMINA* points and then remove it from your list. If you have chosen the walking staff, add 1 *SKILL* point. Unfortunately, the map is exactly the same as the picture stitched into the pall. Turn to **326**.

313

If you have a potion, you may use it. To use 'Thick as Thieves', turn to **386**. To use 'Pretty as a Picture', turn to **399**. To use 'Dragon's Breath', turn to **414**. To try 'Collywobbles', turn to **426**. Or, to try some 'Nostalgia' perfume, turn to **374**. If you have no more potions or do not want to use up any more of your stock, then you will have to fight Blossom – turn to **334**.

A bald, seven-foot-tall brute

314

You sprint away across the fields next to the road, several of the demons coming after you. You sprint faster, but as you get into the next field you run into even more demons. Then, suddenly there's a great roar as some huge creature charges out from a stand of trees and knocks the demons flat.

You stop running. A bald, seven-foot-tall brute with purple and orange skin is laying into the demons with a huge golden blade that has the words 'DEATH TO DEMONS' written on it in what looks like blood. He makes short work of the mob and howls in triumph, wiping his hands on his pink armour.

He sees you looking at him and bows.

'I am Monstroso the Blood Feaster, and I am here to fight,' he says, his voice slurred by a single tusk sticking out of one side of his mouth. 'What are your orders, General? Monstroso need orders. Monstroso not think for himself. Monstroso need fight. Monstroso need kill. Monstroso kill demons. Monstroso HATE demons...'

To tell Monstroso you are trying to get to Broken Goddess Fort, turn to **341**. To thank him for rescuing you and hurry back to the road, turn to **329**.

315

You point your khopesh at the advancing Demon Horde and yell the words, 'Seed of Destruction!' and a swarm of flies buzzes from the tip of the blade and streams across the cavern before tearing into the demons, biting and stinging. More and more flies shoot out and the demons are soon covered with them. They stagger about, flailing, falling, choking as the flies suffocate them and they become a horrible, writhing black mass.

Reduce the *STAMINA* points of the Demon Horde by half.

To fight the horde, turn to **453**. To try more magic, if you have any, turn to **213**.

316

You catch the iron before it can hit you in the head and run out of the door.

Add the fire iron to your Weapons List and turn to **350**.

317

The demons are advancing ever closer up the steps.

Opposite them is an archway leading to an alley. There is no sign of any demons in that direction.

To leap down the steps and take on the demon citizens of Salamonis, turn to **330**. To go through the archway, turn to **343**.

318

You can hear someone – or something – moving about in the house, so you quickly grab the trowel from your pack and desperately start to dig in the soft earth exposed by the fallen statue.

Soon you feel the blade knock against something solid and scrabble in the mud with your fingers before pulling up a small box. You open it to find 25 Gold Pieces. Not exactly a fortune, but enough to buy what you need.

Add the 25 Gold Pieces to your Adventure Sheet and turn to **338**.

319

You walk into the chamber and almost fall headfirst into a glowing purple demon portal in the floor. To try to jump over the portal, turn to **342**. To explore the north chamber, turn to **301**. To leave the chamber and walk down the aisle to the main temple, turn to **387**.

320

You stand up, yawn and stretch out your arms, letting everyone know you're ready for bed. If you want to sleep here, turn to **361**. If you want to try the stable instead, turn to **381**.

321

As you run back towards the fort, arrows clatter down all around you. You feel a sting in your shoulder and see that one has hit you, although the leather strap of your pack has stopped it from penetrating too deeply. You reach the safety of the fortified walls and crouch down to pull the arrow out.

If you have any healing ointment you can use it now and lose no *STAMINA* points, otherwise you will lose 3 *STAMINA* points. Turn to **390**.

322

A building is in flames. It looks like a group of citizens has been trying to put the fire out using flasks of magic firewater, but they are all lying dead in the road. You spot an unused flask of firewater, if you want to, you can pick it up and add it your Equipment List. You are about to explore further when crazed demons rush at you from all sides, screaming. You turn around and run all the way back to Titan Square, leaving them behind. Turn to **149.**

323

The Lamassu turns and heads back towards Salamonis. As you travel, though, you feel that the mighty beast is losing strength and flying slower.

'Those demon swine hurt me worse than I thought,' it says, it's voice croaky. 'I'm not sure how much further I can go with you on my back.'

To look for a place to land nearby, turn to **336**. To urge the Lamassu to press on all the way to Salamonis, turn to **354.**

324

If you have a frog in your pocket, turn to **304**. Otherwise turn to **284.**

325

You search the thieves and find ... three jars of healing ointment, a thieves' skeleton key and 5 Gold Pieces. You may also take one of the thieves' cudgels if you want.

If you want to buy a pie, turn to **265**. If not, turn to **232**.

326

You help the Imps lift Hikaz's body off the bier and lay him gently on the metal plate. Now you wheel the bier away until it is safely out of reach of any flames.

'Three of my Imps will go with you on the bier,' says the King. 'They can take you to the Plain of Bronze and then return here. Meet Oli, Uli and Eli.'

He snaps his fingers and three Imps step forward, salute their King and clamber up on to the bier.

'Look for three mountains standing close to each other,' the King shouts and the Imps nod and chatter in a language you don't understand. To your ears it sounds like parrots laughing.

You get on behind them and see that they're fiddling with some knobs and levers built into the top of the bier. Presently the structure begins to judder and then rise slightly into the air. You grip hold of the sides as the bier wobbles higher. Oli, Uli and Eli are getting very excited and talking even faster as their fingers dart over the controls. Then there's a lurch and you shoot up out of the top of the stone circle. In a moment the bier is flying through the night sky while the three Imps shriek and laugh. One of them, you think it might be Oli, sticks out his tongue and it flaps in the wind.

You watch the stone circle growing smaller and smaller and then you are flying fast across the countryside. Trolltooth Pass is right below you. You follow its route through the Moonstone Hills and as the sun comes up you see that you are flying over endless, featureless steppes. These must be the Flatlands, home to nomadic barbarians. The bier flies on, ever higher and faster as the Imps adjust the controls. Now you see a vast lake away to the east and the land below gets drier and browner as, at last, the vast Plain of Bronze opens out below you.

The Plain is desolate and dry, covered with dark red sand and ash embedded with glinting lumps of bronze in all shapes and sizes. Here and there are the ruins of ancient settlements that are slowly being swallowed up by the sand. The sun is at its highest by the time you spot the three peaks, which look more like tall pillars of rock than mountains. You head towards them and then circle around them for a while, but can see no signs of any city. The three peaks are all slightly different colours. One is reddish brown, one is a sandy colour and the third one is ash grey. The top of each rock is only about the size of the roof of a house.

You remember the pictures on the pall. If you have the adventurer's bronze star, turn to **348**. Otherwise choose which pillar of rock you want to land the bier on. To land on the red one, turn to **362**. To land on the sandy one, turn to **375**. To land on the grey one, turn to **388**.

327

It takes nearly all night for you to reach the burial grounds, and you are exhausted by the time you get there. (Lose 1 *STAMINA* point.)

You eventually see some grave markers and mausoleums on either side of the track and finally, ahead of you, you see a circle of mighty stones, black against the starry sky. There are coloured lights blazing inside the circle and a pillar of coloured smoke rises up to the heavens. Turn to **137.**

328

Bad choice. The bolt strikes you and your body is blasted into a million pieces.

Your adventure is over.

You manage to get past the demon farmers and hurry on down the road towards Trolltooth Pass, running as fast as the swift silver boots will carry you. You're just thinking you are out of danger when you hear a thundering sound behind you and throw yourself to the side of the road, narrowly avoiding being run down by Lady Webspinn's driverless carriage. As it rattles past you, you see that it's being drawn by four demon horses.

You dust yourself down and run after it. Soon you see the low hills that mark the entrance to Trolltooth Pass, which will lead you to the Plain of Bronze. You hardly tire at all, and as night falls you are still running. At some point you fall asleep, but still the boots keep on running. When you wake the next morning you find that you are deep in Trolltooth Pass, with high cliffs on either side of you and still running.

You are growing weary, however, and feel your strength dimming. (Lose 1 *STAMINA* point.) You slow down and tramp on, hardly noticing your surroundings, and as the sun starts to dip in the sky you at last see a huge statue of the Goddess Sindla standing atop the cliffs on the northern side of the pass. Part of its head and torso are missing along with its right arm. Next to it are some ramparts and a crumbling lookout tower. Below it, by the side of the road, are the remains of a lower fort, tangled with weeds and thorn bushes.

You have made it to Broken Goddess Fort. As you get closer you see the wreck of Lady Webspinn's carriage that must have crashed into the cliffs. You sit down, exhausted. Your boots are in tatters from running so far, and you take them off and throw them away (remove them from your Equipment List). To explore the surrounding area, turn to **282**. To go into the fort, turn to **390.**

330
You feel yourself falling and then you land with a thump. Once you've regained your senses you see that you're surrounded by the demon citizens of Salamonis. These who were once bankers, bakers, butchers, builders, merchants, washerwomen, fine lords and ladies are now monstrous things from a nightmare… You close your eyes, not wanting to see the claws and teeth, the carving knives and mallets and clubs that are coming down towards your head.

Your adventure is over.

331
'I learnt about the book from an adventurer who I … had an argument with,' says Sinna. 'He lost the argument. It is called *The Book of the Dead*. It's here in the Great

Library of Throff somewhere and tells you how to pass safely through the gates. I looked for it, but the library is enchanted and I never found it. Perhaps you will have more luck…'

If you have the Book of the Dead, turn to **217**. To ask Sinna about the khopesh, turn to **285**. To return to the refectory, turn to **460**. To try the rings in the Gates of Death, turn to **356**.

332

You hurry back into the circle of light. You feel safe here with Brother Tobyn, but it's clear that he's not well. The wound that the monstrous merchant gave him has become infected and is starting to fester. The old Guardian is feverish and you can't get him to talk to you. Without the items in your backpack, there's nothing you can do for him, so you make him as comfortable as you can and settle down for the night. Turn to **413**.

333

'They truly are beautiful maps,' says Swann. 'They were drawn by the finest mapmaker in all Titan, Master Evett Luxtonas. But I fear you won't be able to afford them. If you have 200 Gold Pieces, however, they are yours.'

If you have 200 Gold Pieces, turn to **351**. If you don't have enough Pieces, turn to **364**.

A huge, hairy mutant with four arms

334

DEMONIC BLOSSOM shrieks and rushes at you, waving the pig's jawbone.

DEMONIC BLOSSOM   *SKILL 6*   *STAMINA 8*

If you win, turn to **345**.

335

You hurry into the cave and immediately realize you've made a mistake. There's a creature of some sort in here and you've disturbed it. It lumbers towards you out of the shadows and you see it's a CLAWBEAST, a huge, hairy mutant with four arms, each one tipped with a long claw.

The Clawbeast blocks the cave entrance and lashes out at you with all four claws. There's no time to use any magic, so you will have to fight it.

CLAWBEAST   *SKILL 8*   *STAMINA 9*

If you win, turn to **353**.

336

You are flying over Trolltooth Pass, but now night has fallen and you can see very little, except there, on a high plateau in the cliffs above the pass, what looks like a stone circle with coloured fire burning inside it. You tell the Lamassu to go down for a closer look and pass over the ruins of a fort where there a lookout tower, a broken statue, and some huts, with smoke rising from the roof of one. To bid farewell to the Lamassu and ask him to set you down by the fort, turn to **408**. To bid farewell and ask him to set you down near the stone circle, turn to **137**.

337

The iron hits you in the head, sending you reeling. (Lose 2 *STAMINA* points.) Feeling dizzy and groggy, you stagger out of the door.

Add the fire iron to your Weapons List and turn to **350**.

338

You stand up and brush dirt off your clothing. And it's then that you hear the sound of smashing glass and see a terrible sight. Demons are running out of the house, pouring out through the door and jumping down from the broken windows. You run back to the gates and desperately clamber up the gatepost. When you get to the top, however, a demon hurls a brick that hits you on the head.

Lose 2 *STAMINA* points and 1 *SKILL* point. You will regain these points at the end of the next battle you fight, by which time your head should have cleared.

You stand there wobbling. Which way will you fall? Into the street or back into the garden? If you have a trowel, turn to **379**. Otherwise you will have to *Test your Luck*, turn to **359**.

339

The arrow hits you and you fall to the ground. As you land, the contents of your pack spill out. You pull out the arrow but feel your life force ebbing away. You wonder if there's anything among your items that could help you.

If you have any healing ointment turn to **358**. Otherwise, if you have the brass compass, turn to **346**. Or if you have a bottle of 'Nostalgia', turn to **442**. If there's nothing useful in your Equipment List, turn to **378**.

340

'We wish you luck,' says the half-elf when you have told them your story. 'We believe the plague is spreading from the Plain of Bronze where the Invisible City lies. If you travel there, make sure you have a map and some means of seeing the city. And take this, it may come in useful.'

The half-elf hands you a jar of healing ointment. Add it to your Equipment List and then turn to **320**.

341

'Monstroso help,' says the bald giant. 'You want horse? Monstroso have horse. Monstroso was going to eat horse, but if great general wants horse, great general have horse.'

So saying, Monstroso leads you over to the stand of trees where there's a horse lying on its back with its legs tied together. He unties it and, once it has struggled back on to its feet, you mount it.

'Trolltooth Pass very dangerous,' says Monstroso. 'Full of bad men and monsters and demons. Monstroso hate demons. Monstroso know back way through Moonstone Hills, though. Monstroso not stupid. Well, Monstroso bit stupid. You follow.'

And so the big bald idiot sets off running. He moves

surprisingly fast and even on horseback you struggle to keep up with him. To the north you see the entrance to Trolltooth Pass, but Monstroso takes a track that goes up into the hills on the south side. You travel all day and most of the night, only resting for a while to eat and grab a few precious moments of sleep. At dawn, Monstroso is off and running again. The path he's taking you along winds higher and higher as the hills become jagged peaks. Towards the end of the day, he starts to lead you down towards the pass.

'Fort near,' he says. 'Go careful. Pass dangerous.'

Indeed, the words are hardly out of his mouth when you spot a goblin raiding party scouting along the top of the pass.

'Goblins!' says Monstroso. 'Monstroso hate Goblins nearly as much as Monstroso hate demons! You go. Monstroso stay fight. Monstroso lives to fight.'

He points the way down into the pass and you hurry on. Behind you, you can hear Monstroso roaring a battle cry and the shouts of startled Goblins. On the cliffs on the far side of the pass, you can see a huge statue of the Goddess Sindla. Half its head and torso are missing along with its right arm. Next to it are some ramparts and a crumbling lookout tower. Below it, on the northern side of the road are the remains of a lower fort, tangled with weeds and thorn bushes.

You climb the rest of the way down the cliff to the pass and hurry over to the fort. Turn to **390.**

342

You jump across the portal – but not far enough, and you tumble into the pool of purple light, which sucks you deeper and deeper into the demonic realm.

You learnt a spell to escape from a danger such as this. Will you get it right? To chant the words 'Exitus, exodus, excitus...' Turn to **360**. To chant the words 'Execrus, exodus, exitus...' turn to **367**. To chant the words 'Excitus, exitus, exodus...' Turn to **373**.

343

You run through the arch into the alleyway. It turns sharply left and as you career around the corner you see, too late, a strange glowing pool of purple light in the ground, out of which two disembodied demon spirits are emerging, looking for a body to infect. Your only chance of escape is to throw yourself into the pool.

You know that this must be a demon portal, one of the

places where the demon spirits are coming into this world. It's like diving into a strong current. You are going against the flow of magic and are quickly lost in space and time. With all your mental strength, you reach back out to the real world, and you dimly recall the words of a spell. Can you remember them correctly?

Turn to **355**.

344

'You want to know about the young adventurer?' says Swann. 'He was from the Icefinger Mountains and was desperate to find the Invisible City. He was sure that the demon plague was spreading from there. I sold him my best map of the Plain of Bronze. Much good will it do him. The thing about the Invisible City is that, well, it's invisible! So it's not marked on any map. He had an idea, though, that he could find out more about the Invisible City in the burial grounds near the ruins of Broken Goddess Fort, halfway along Trolltooth Pass. So he was heading that way. He sold me a box of his, sealed by magic. It was no use to him any longer as he'd lost the key when he was locked up for a spell in Lord Azzur's dungeons.'

To ask to see the adventurer's box, turn to **324**. To ask to look at what else Swann can offer you, turn to **364**.

345

'What have you done?' shouts Fossick, who has been watching everything through the trapdoor. 'I didn't ask you to kill my only daughter! You're more of a monster than she was. You can rot down there ... for ever!'

So saying, he slams the trapdoor shut. You can hear him dragging the heavy treasure chest back on to it. The lamp burns out and you alone are in the darkness with Blossom's corpse.

Your adventure is over.

346

Your hand closes on the compass you picked up in the Fish Market. And as you stare at it, the pointer spins round and you feel the whole world spinning with it... *Test your Luck*. If you are Lucky, turn to **365**. If you are Unlucky, turn to **462**.

347

You've had enough of being pushed around in Port Blacksand. You square up to the two THIEVES and fight them one after the other.

	SKILL	STAMINA
First THIEF	7	6
Second THIEF	6	7

If you win, turn to **325**.

348

While you've been flying, you've been studying the funeral bier more closely, and have spotted a carved-out shape that matches the shape of the bronze star. You take the star out of your pack and find that it fits perfectly into the carved space. As it slots into place it lights up, glowing bright blue. And as you look down you now see a glowing blue star on top of the grey pillar of rock.

To land on the grey rock, turn to **388**. Or if you want to land on the red one, turn to **362**. To land on the sandy one, turn to **375**.

349

Once more you avoid Ulrakaah's attack and this time you sink the blade in up to its hilt, and when you tug it free there is a gush of blood like a waterfall. Turn to **78**.

350

It's raining harder than ever outside the cottage and you're exhausted. To inspect the barn, turn to **184**. To hide in the woodshed and try to get some sleep, turn to **203**.

351

There's a flash of light and the shop is suddenly filled with smoke. A familiar figure emerges out of the gloom. It's the Trickster God, Logaan, himself. He points a bony finger at you and cackles, 'Liar, liar, pants on fire!' Suddenly your pants catch fire and you run screaming all the way back to Titan Square.

Lost 3 *STAMINA* points and turn to **149**.

Your situation is desperate. You'll take all the help you can get. You inch forward until your hands touch skin ... hair ... an ear... You freeze and hear a chuckle in the darkness.

'It's all right.' The voice is so weak you can hardly hear it. 'I'm not going to hurt you. We're all in the stew together. I have something for you...'

You hear a hiss of breath and then see a patch of greenish-blue light start to glow on the wall. It looks like it's coming from a patch of fungus. There's another hiss of breath and the fungus glows brighter.

'It's glow-mould,' says the voice. 'It feeds on your breath.'

As the fungus glows slowly brighter you are gradually able to make out the figure of a man chained to the wall. He's terribly thin, his skin covered in sores and blisters and there's an awful rotting smell coming off him.

'I haven't got long to live,' he whispers, and his chest rattles as he draws in another breath. 'I've kept a treasure with me here. The gaolers never found it ... but I'm dying now and have to pass it on to someone... You might be able to use it...'

'What is it?'

'A special key ... left here by an adventurer from the Icefinger Mountains. Hidden in one of my boots... It's yours now...'

'What's it for?' you ask. 'Where can I use it? Which boot?' But the man is silent and the fungus is losing its glow. The poor prisoner has breathed his last.

You can just see a pair of boots standing next to him. You're going to have to search them. But can you trust the prisoner? Perhaps he wanted to play a trick on you.

If you want to try the right boot, turn to **372**. If you want to try the left boot, turn to **392**. If you want to hurry back to Brother Tobyn, turn to **332**.

353

You manage to strike the Clawbeast down and then quickly explore its cave. You discover a dead traveller in the back, and in his pack you find a bronze compass, a bottle of 'Pretty as a Picture' potion, a flask of firewater and a cold sausage. (The sausage will restore up to 2 *STAMINA* points, whether you eat it now or later.) You take the items, leave the cave and run back to the fort, turn to **321**.

354

Wearily, the Lamassu flies on towards Salamonis, using the thermal currents above the hills to circle higher and higher and then glide down so that it can rest its wings. At last the walls of the ancient city come into view.

'I will set you down on a rooftop,' says the mighty creature. 'And then I will leave you. I cannot risk staying there when I am so weak. Watch out for demons. They are dangerous, unless you can catch hold of one and tether it. A tethered demon must always do your bidding. And watch out for the portals that they have opened to enter our world. If you do fall into one, remember the words, "Exitus, exodus, excitus…"'

He flies down towards the buildings in a wide circle, selects a rooftop and lands gently. You slip off his back and thank him. In a moment he is airborne again and you watch him fly off southwards. Turn to **227.**

355

To chant the words 'Execrus, exodus, exitus', turn to **394.**
To chant the words 'Excitus, exitus, exodus', turn to **367.**
To chant the words 'Exitus, exodus, excitus', turn to **380.**

'We are the Guardians of the Gates'

356

You step forward and take hold of one of the rings, trying to ignore the hideous screaming faces and skeletal hands that try to grab hold of you. As you lift the ring and turn it, you hear a heavy thumping, cracking sound, like huge rocks knocking together, and then see two dark shapes rising from the floor. They are giant guards made of black crystal. Bodies, armour, halberds, helmets with closed visors, all are formed from gleaming obsidian. Their heavy crystal boots shake the ground as they stomp towards you.

'We are the Guardians of the Gates,' they say in unison, their voices sounding as if they have come down to you over the years from centuries ago. They raise their halberds.

To fight the OBSIDIAN GIANTS, choose a weapon and turn to **210**. To flee back to the refectory, turn to **460**.

357

'You're not getting out of there until you've fixed my lovely Blossom!' Fossick shouts.

To fight Blossom, turn to **334**. To use a vial of smoke-oil, turn to **438**. To try a magic potion, if you have any, turn to **313**.

358

You take some ointment from the jar and rub it on your wound.

You lose 1 *STAMINA* point, unless this would take your *STAMINA* score to 0, in which case leave it at 1 point.

After a while the wound has healed and you are well enough to carry on. Thanking the powers of magic, you throw the empty jar away and walk on, using the high corn to keep you hidden. Once you're sure it's safe, you leave the field and join an old herders' track. Turn to **159**.

359

Test your Luck. If you are Lucky, you fall into the street, turn to **379**. If you are Unlucky, you fall into the garden, turn to **330**.

360

You remembered the spell correctly. The portal spits you out and you find yourself in the Temple Gardens. Turn to **275**.

361

You pay the landlord 1 Gold Piece and he shows you to your room, which is small but clean.

'My rooster will wake you at daybreak,' he says and leaves you to settle down for a good night's sleep.

Add 2 *STAMINA* points and turn to **109**.

362

The bier zooms round the top of the red rock in ever-tightening circles and then swoops in and lands with a bump. Oli, Eli and Uli hug each other and give a little dance of joy. You climb off the bier and look around. You are just about to thank the Imps and ask them to wait when you realize that they've already taken off and are circling the rock again. You shout at them to come back, but it's no good; they fly off, madly chattering. Turn to **427**.

363

If you have any of the following items listed on your Adventure Sheet, cross them off now:

Temple Guard's Axe, Flea Boots, any Magical Seeds, Cookbook, *Hither Chaos Angel Died*, Bronze-Coloured Jewel, Weakwater.

Your Provisions, Gold Pieces and any potions you possess are unaffected by the strange magic. However, as you travel back in time, the smoke-oil you lost to Denka Mansell is restored to you.

Restore your *SKILL*, *STAMINA* and *LUCK* scores to their Initial values and turn to **275**.

364

What are you interested in buying from Sandford Swann?

To buy the map of Salamonis, turn to **403**. For the map of Trolltooth Pass, turn to **383**. If you want the set of three maps, turn to **333**.

Or, to ask about the adventurer who was here before you, turn to **344**. If you want to ask Swann to show you his equipment for explorers, turn to **20**. To ask to look at his magic items, turn to **36**. If you want to ask him where you can get more money, turn to **55**. If you want to leave the shop, turn to **103.**

365

Time begins to run backwards. You realize that the compass is magic and has the power to return you to an earlier point in time and space. You will be able to relive part of your adventure... Turn to **14**.

The Obsidian Giants strike you down with their crystal halberds. You experience a moment of searing pain and then nothing. You have lost all feeling in your body, and as it hits the floor your spirit lifts free. The giants freeze and you can see a black khopesh hanging in the air where it is embedded in one of the gates, which have become transparent and hazy. You can just make out a large open space on the other side. Your spirit drifts over towards the gates, floating in the air, and now it passes through them and you are in the realm of the dead.

You find yourself in a cavern similar to the one you have just left, with weirdly-coloured crystals glowing in its walls. On the ground are heaps of dead warriors. You see disembodied spirits like yourself searching among the bodies, their faces masks of agony and sorrow. You choose a powerful-looking warrior, well clad in armour, and your spirit enters the corpse. It feels strange to be in another's body, but it also feels powerful. You rise up, strong and alive and bursting with energy. (Return your *STAMINA* score to its Initial level.)

All your senses have returned, and the first thing that hits you is the stink of this place, like a cesspit filled with filth. You try to ignore it as you go over to the gates, which now appear solid again. On this side they are smooth and shiny and you can see your reflection in them. You see the blade of the black khopesh sticking out. You know that without one of these enchanted blades you can never defeat Ulrakaah. To try to pull the black khopesh through to this side, turn to **397**. If you already have a khopesh, turn to **457.**

367

You got the spell wrong… You feel yourself thrown around by the forces inside the portal until at last you are spat out at the other end. You land with a thump and lie there for a moment, winded. When you are finally able to get up you take a look around. You are in some kind of vast underground cavern, the walls aglow with yellow, green and purple crystals. You see a group of hideously deformed demons lumbering towards you, and then feel a hot wind on your neck. You turn around to find yourself face to face with a giant female monster, leering down at you. She has the face of a corpse, rotting and green, with dead eyes. She opens her mouth wide, exposing two rows of sharp, snaggly yellow teeth.

'Ulrakaah,' she hisses, and then she bites…

Your adventure is over.

368

You raise your blade to strike the creature and … it jumps up and turns around. You're amazed to see that it's not a monster at all, but a young acolyte like yourself.

'Please don't hurt me!' the acolyte bleats and you put your weapon away. 'My name is Castrabel, and I was praying. All the others have gone, but I stayed. I thought my prayers might help. I'm wearing a cloak of protection. If you look at it from behind, it appears to be the face of a monster. Castrabel turns around again and you see that the hideous creature is only a magical moving image on the cloak.

'Until now it has scared everyone else away,' Castrabel says. 'Who are you that is brave enough to fight such a thing? Have you come to save us?'

To ask Castrabel where the High Priestess is, turn to **384**. To ask about the Gates of Death, turn to **423**. To ask about the temple, turn to **440**. To return to the dormitory, turn to **295**.

369

You push Nicodemus aside, grab Brother Tobyn and hurry out of the hut, all the while expecting Nicodemus to hurl some magic after you. You remember his directions and start running up Bridge Street, but now the shady characters hanging out on the street corners are no longer ignoring the two of you. In ones and twos they break away and start to follow you, and, before you're even halfway to the Market Square, two men grab you and pull you into a pie shop.

'Congratulations,' says one of them, a weaselly little creep with no teeth, and he gives a low, sarcastic, bow. 'You've fallen into the hands of the Guild of Thieves, and we have stolen you. We know some people who'd pay the price of a good pie for a Guardian and his acolyte. It'll save us the bother of having to steal one.'

If you want to fight the two THIEVES, turn to **347**. If you'd rather not risk it and see where this takes you, turn to **305**.

370

No matter how hard you pull on their reins or how loudly you shout at the horses, they won't stop. Suddenly, you hear a crack and the whole carriage jars before tipping over sideways. You are thrown clear and watch as it crashes into the cliff face. (Lose 3 *STAMINA* points.) You manage to stand up and limp back to the fort. Turn to **390**.

371

You have defeated the Bum-Faced Monster. It dissolves into a puddle of purple liquid that quickly turns to smoke, leaving behind a cold sausage, a cookbook and a bottle of 'Nostalgia'. Take what you want and then, to go through the door with the moon symbol, turn to **299**. To go through the door that looks like a book, turn to **192**. To go through the door to the Walkway of Evening, turn to **84**.

372

You slip your hand inside the right boot and wince as you touch something cold and wet, but before you can pull your hand away it goes numb and an icy pain shoots up your arm. When you do finally manage to get your hand out of the boot you've lost all feeling in it and can see a huge, slug-like dungeon crawler attached to your skin by its teeth, sucking hard. The thing is glowing slightly with the same green light as the fungus. It is white and blind and almost transparent from living in the darkness, and you can see your blood inside it, filling it up.

You smash it against the wall and it lets go of your hand and falls to the floor, oozing cold slime and warm blood.

(You lose 3 *STAMINA* points and 2 *SKILL* points.) If you

want to try your luck with the left boot, turn to **392**. If you want to hurry back to Brother Tobyn, turn to **332.**

373

You know immediately that you got the spell wrong, but you have learnt much from your adventures. You will now do battle with the goddess Sindla, the Goddess of Luck, to see what happens next.

Roll two dice. If you roll a 2 or a 12, she sends you to **367**. If you roll a 3 or an 11, she sends you to **394**. If you roll any other number, the portal will spit you out, turn to **275.**

374

You open the 'Nostalgia' perfume bottle and a smell of pears wafts out. You feel your whole world spinning... Time seems to run backwards... You realize the potion will allow you to relive part of your adventure... But how far back will it take you? Turn to **14**.

375

The Imps steer towards the sandy-coloured rock, but they're going too fast and the bier is out of control. It crashes into the side of the rock and you are tipped off. You just manage to grab hold of a sticking-out crag and haul yourself up on to the top of the rock. The bier flies around crazily and then zooms away. Turn to **447.**

He has a round, sweaty face and a small goatee beard

376

'Greetings,' says the man. 'I am the Holy Man. Like you, I came here to help cleanse Allansia of the demon plague. To defeat Ulrakaah needs skills in both magic and combat. I have magic but I cannot take up arms – it is not in my nature. You, however, have learnt much in your adventures. Are you willing to take the fight to the mother of demons beyond the Gates of Death?'

To ask about Ulrakaah, turn to **452**. To ask about the Gates of Death, turn to **439**. To return to the tunnel, turn to **147.**

377

You hear a rattling of locks and chains and at last the door is opened by the man wearing the helmet.

'Come in, quickly,' he says and you don't wait to be told twice. Once inside he bolts the door behind you. 'So you've come all the way from the Crucible Isles to save us, have you?' he says, taking off the helmet. 'You're not the first – there was a young adventurer in here just a few days ago – but I fear you may be the last.'

He's a large man who looks like he enjoys his food. He has a round, sweaty face and a small goatee beard.

'Pleased to meet you,' he says, offering you a damp hand to shake. 'My name is Sandford Swann and this shop has been in my family for twenty generations. Whether it will survive this demon curse, I don't know. I have these big brutes to protect me.' He nods towards the Man-Orcs who grunt at you but say nothing. 'There are more demons on the streets every day,' Swann goes on, looking out of the window. 'I sometimes think I'm the last uninfected person left in Salamonis... So, what can I do for you? I have locked most of my maps away in a safe place to stop them from being destroyed, but I do have a few left here in the shop. I have a good map of Salamonis, a map of Trolltooth Pass, and I have a lovely set of three maps showing Allansia, the Old World and Khul. I also sell equipment for explorers and even have a few magic items.'

If you want to leave the shop, turn to **103**. Otherwise, turn to **364**.

378

Without the means to reverse its effects, the wound soon proves fatal and your adventure is over.

379

You jump down and land safely in the street. The demons scream across the garden behind you and start to climb the gates. You turn and leg it all the way back to Titan Square. Turn to **149**.

380

You got the spell right, but where will you emerge? You are in the hands of Sindla, Goddess of Fortune.

Roll two dice. If you roll a 2 or a 12, turn to **100**. If you roll a 3 or an 11, turn to **149**. If you roll any other number, turn to **200**.

381

The night sky is cloudy and it's drizzling. You hurry into the stable and climb into the hayloft where you bed down in a pile of straw, covering yourself with handfuls of it so that you are well hidden.

It has been a long day and you soon fall asleep. (Add 1 *STAMINA* point.)

You are dreaming of demons and magic when a movement wakes you. You open your eyes and look around. The clouds must have gone because a thin chink of moonlight is shining through a hole in the roof and falling across the straw. You wonder what it was that woke you and then sense something moving around inside your tunic. You feel it take hold of your purse and tug at it.

You jump up and gingerly stick your hand inside your tunic where you grab hold of whatever it is. It feels like a man's forearm, warm and hairless, but there's nobody else here. You drag it out and hold it up, squirming and spitting. It's a fat, pink, naked creature with unseeing eyes and five groping tentacles fanning out around its mouth, like fingers. If it weren't for the eyes you'd think you actually were holding a man's severed arm. You have heard about these creatures that steal things in the night, but never seen one before. It's a HAY THIEVER.

You hurl it down to the stable floor where it lays for a moment, stunned, before starting to slither away like a huge, fat slug. To let it go, turn to **401**. To try to kill it, turn to **431**. To follow it, turn to **451**.

382

Your khopesh is pulsating with stored power. You aim it towards the advancing Demon Horde, yell the words, 'Seed of Doubt!' and silver fire spurts out, washing over them. The effect is immediate, many of the demons instantly lose the will to fight and drop their weapons, but not all ... some are still willing to battle on.

Reduce the *STAMINA* points of the Demon Horde by half. Reduce their *SKILL* points by half.

To fight the horde, turn to **453**. To try more magic, if you have any, turn to **213**.

383

'This is a very simple, but accurate map of how to get from Salamonis to Trolltooth Pass,' says Swann, showing you a rolled map in a tube. 'It also shows some of the Plain Of Bronze. It's yours for 5 Gold Pieces. If you don't have the money I can tell you where to find some, if you like.'

To buy the map, pay 5 Gold Pieces. To view it, make a note of this section number and turn to **173**. When you have looked at it turn back here and make sure to mark the number **173** next to your map in your Equipment List in case you ever want to look at it again.

To ask about where to find more money, turn to **55**. Otherwise, turn to **364**.

384

'When we realized that Ulrakaah was sending her demonic forces out through the portals to attack us,' says Castrabel, 'the High Priestess hid everyone in the city. She has placed them on another plane where they are safe for now, but it has left the city vulnerable and all sorts of monsters have got in. The High Priestess is still here, however, hiding in a secret chamber behind the shrine of Lunara in the main temple. If you give the correct offering to Lunara, the concealed door will open.'

To ask Castrabel about the Gates of Death, turn to **423**. To ask about the temple, turn to **234**. To return to the dormitory, turn to **295**.

385

You walk down the steps and find that they lead to a bathhouse. There are jars of oils and salts and scented herbs. Steam is rising from a big bath of warm water fed by a hot spring. To take a bath, turn to **461**. To go back to the passageway, turn to **279**.

386

You open the 'Thick as Thieves' potion jar and nasty, blue smoke drifts out. Blossom takes one sniff of it and burps louder than before, but she's otherwise unaffected.

Cross the 'Thick as Thieves' potion off your Adventure Sheet and turn to **313**.

387

You come into the main Temple Of Throff, where there's a huge statue of the goddess, standing in the middle under the dome. It is made of pure silver and the sunlight streaming in through the high windows in the dome make it glow.

The temple is circular, with pillars holding up the dome, which is painted to look like the sky. There are images of clouds, birds and the sun on one side, and stars, planets and the moon on the other. There are walkways going off through archways to north and south. The walkway to the north has a pale blue tiled floor and lettering above the archway tells you it is the Walkway of Day; the other one, going south, has dark blue tiles and is called the Walkway of Night.

You look around, wondering where you might find the High Priestess. This place is as deserted as everywhere else. You find a patch of dried blood and some broken pottery. You also find some scattered pages from a book, written in a language you cannot understand. Behind the statue of Throff against the western wall, you find a small shrine to the moon goddess, Lunara. You know that some people pray to her to find things that have been lost and there is an offering bowl in front of the statue. Turn to **406**.

388

The bier lands with a mighty bone-shaking thump on top of the grey rock. For a moment the three Imps are too stunned to even move and, for the first time since you set off, they are silent. And then suddenly they are jumping up and down in triumph and hugging each other. You get off the bier, glad to have your feet on solid rock.

You look out across the endless Plain of Bronze, baking under a hot sun. There is no sign of any city. You hear a noise above you like chattering birds and look up to see that the Imps have taken off. You watch helplessly as they fly off home, madly gabbling away to each other.

You remember the picture stitched into the pall. The man standing on one of these rocks was wearing goggles. If you have the bier goggles, turn to **404**. Otherwise, turn to **416.**

389

The Holy Man leans forward and pops a seed out from a hole in the end of one finger ... and then another from a hole in his arm, and yet another from his stomach... Soon there are several seeds in front of him: three Seeds of Mastery, three Seeds of Power, one Seed of Knowledge, a Seed of Doubt, a Seed of Treachery, a Seed of Destruction, and one Seed of Change.

Pick up the seeds you want and reduce your *STAMINA* by 1 point for each one taken. Be careful not to go below 1 *STAMINA* point, though, or you will die and it will all be over.

Once you have the seeds you want you can use them whenever you wish. Each Seed of Mastery you take from the Holy Man will immediately add 1 to your *SKILL* score. Each Seed of Strength will add 1 to your *STAMINA* score, whenever you eat it.

To ask the Holy Man about Ulrakaah, turn to **452**. To ask him about the Gates of Death, turn to **439**. To return to the tunnel, turn to **147**.

390

You enter the fort, where you find a keep built into the cliff wall. The gates and roof have long since rotted away. You enter the walls and find a stairway leading up inside the solid rock. You climb it to the top and come out by the watchtower. Turn to **408**.

'What have we here?' says the male face, its grin growing wider.

'Lunch,' says the female face.

'Looks too stringy to me,' says the first.

'You're too fussy. You're a really fussy eater.'

'At least I'm not ugly.'

'I am NOT ugly,' says the second.

'Have you seen yourself lately?' says the man. 'You've got a face like a bum...'

While they are arguing you have the chance to grab a temple guard's axe if you want to. Otherwise, choose another weapon from your list and make ready to fight the BUM-FACED MONSTER.

BUM-FACED MONSTER   *SKILL 8*   *STAMINA 12*

If you win, turn to **371**.

392

You are cautious. There could be anything in the boot. You pick it up, turn it upside down and shake it. There's a tinkling sound and the glint of metal. You scrabble in the dirt and pick up the Icefinger Key and hide it in your own boot. Perhaps the prisoner had more hidden treasure?

Add the Icefinger Key to your Equipment List. If you haven't already done so, do you want to try your luck with the right boot? If so, turn to **372**. If you want to hurry back to Brother Tobyn, turn to **332**.

393

You try the door. It's locked. A horrible grunting, hissing noise warns you that some demons have sniffed you out and are advancing along the street behind you. You hammer on the door and hear a muffled voice on the other side.

'Go away.'

To explain who you are and what you are doing, turn to **377**. To try to break the door down, turn to **136**. To run back the way you came, turn to **108**.

394

You are trapped in the portal, neither in the demonic plane nor the real world, lost in time and space. You will spin on here in this purple void for all eternity...

Your adventure is over.

395

You head down the road. There's a noise like marching feet behind you, but you are moving at speed and can't see anybody. You come to a crossroads.

To go east, turn to **16**. To go down the street heading south, turn to **465**. To go down the street heading north, turn to **415**. To go west towards Titan Square, turn to **149**.

396

The arrow flies past your ear and hits a scarecrow. Thanking Sindla, the Goddess of Luck, you run on, using the high corn to keep you hidden. Once you're sure it's safe, you leave the field and join an old herders' track. Turn to **159**.

There is a man sitting cross-legged on the floor

397

You take hold of the blade and tug it – the khopesh slips through the door like a knife through butter. There are glowing splashes on the steel where it has been washed with a magical liquid of some sort. You recognize the distinct smell of 'Pretty as a Picture' potion. Now you are armed with an enchanted weapon and ready to take on Ulrakaah. (If you have a different khopesh, you can choose to use either one.) Turn to **457**.

398

The hole in the wall leads into a small cave, lit by glowing green and red crystals embedded in the walls. There is a man sitting cross-legged on the floor with a pulsating blue orb suspended above his head. He is wearing only an old grey loincloth and you see that his skin is covered with holes, inside each one of which sits what looks like a large seed about the size of a pea. You understand now why he's called the Holy Man.

He smiles at you. To ask him who he is, turn to **376**. To choose some of the Holy Man's seeds, turn to **389**. To back out through the hole, turn to **147**.

399

You open the 'Pretty as a Picture' potion jar and turquoise-coloured smoke that smells of lavender wafts out. Blossom breathes some in and her smile grows even wider.

'Oh, look at me, look at me,' she cries. 'I'm the prettiest girl in all the world! How lucky you are to be killed and eaten by someone so beautiful!'

Cross the 'Pretty as a Picture' potion off your Adventure Sheet and turn to **313**.

400

You feel the power of the khopesh coursing through your body. You are strong, terrifyingly strong. Maybe one day you will be as powerful as Ulrakaah... You are the ruler of this realm now. You will remain here for ever ... or until another comes to destroy you.

Your adventure is over.

401

The hayloft feels warm and safe. You cover yourself with straw and, clutching your purse tightly, settle back down to sleep, remembering now that Hay Thievers are pretty harmless. Turn to **109**.

402

'I have brought some magic Seeds of Galana to the temple,' says the Holy Man. 'Each one will give you different abilities. But I warn you now, there is a price. Each seed you take from me will reduce your strength, so choose wisely. I have Seeds of Knowledge that allow you to speak and understand any language, but not read it. I have Seeds of Doubt that cause any enemy to lose the will to fight. I have Seeds of Treachery that cause enemies to turn against each other. I have Seeds of Mastery that boost your fighting skills, even beyond their normal levels. And I have Seeds of Power that make you stronger. Also, I would advise you to find some of the magic potion called 'Pretty as a Picture' and take it with you if you can. There should be some here in the temple potions room. There are also two magic pools. One of them will increase your strength if you need it, and the other will decrease it.'

To choose some of the Holy Man's seeds, turn to **389**. To ask him about Ulrakaah, turn to **452**. To ask him about the Gates of Death, turn to **439**. To return to the tunnel, turn to **147.**

403

'I'd love to take all your money, but a map of Salamonis is of no use to you now,' says Swann. 'I can tell you how to get out of town. Simply go back up the street that brought you here, turn right at the top into the North Road and carry straight on south down to Titan Square, then take the East Road straight up to the East Gate, where you'll find the road for Trolltooth Pass.' Turn to **364.**

404

You slip on the bier goggles and immediately everything looks different. You feel as if you are looking at a vision. The plain is no longer a desert of ash and bronze. It's covered in lush green grass, and trees, and rivers. There are farms and villages, crops growing in fields, animals grazing... It looks like a perfect wonderland. And there, standing in the middle of all this bounty, is a beautiful city, rising up, the buildings all whitewashed, with blue tiled roofs. You see fountains and gardens and walkways and at the top, a great silver dome.

And as you look at your feet, you see steps spiralling down the grey rock towards a road that leads to the city. You climb down the steps to the bottom and walk along the road. The only thing missing from the idyllic scenes all around you are people.

In no time at all you arrive at the city, which has no walls or gates. You enter a small square, take off the bier goggles and look back at the way you came. The green fields and rivers and villages have disappeared. You are sure now that you were seeing an image of how this land was a very long time ago, before some awful catastrophe befell it. Now all is barren desert. You turn away and walk deeper into the city. Turn to **21**.

405

You pick up Fossick's axe. (Add the woodman's axe to your Weapons List.) Ignoring the noises from the cellar, which are growing louder and louder, you go over to the treasure chest and inspect it. It's locked with a weird-looking device in the shape of a dragon. You fiddle with it but then jump back as the device glows red hot and the chest shakes violently, knocking into a bookcase. A book falls off a shelf and you pick it up – it's a book of love poetry. (Add the book of love poetry to your Equipment List.)

You know that Fossick's chest is full of treasure, but the lock must be enchanted and will be difficult to open. To hurry out of the cottage and get on with your quest, turn to **350**. To try to open the chest, turn to **417**.

406

You are in the heart of the Temple. The great silver statue of the goddess Throff stands before you. To take the Walkway of Day to the north, turn to **190**. To take the Walkway of Night to the south, turn to **38**. To go down the Aisle of Guardians to the east, turn to **288**. To make an offering to the goddess Lunara by the west wall, turn to **422**.

407

The man with the demon dogs looks at you with sad, frightened eyes.

'Will you help me?' he croaks. 'I'll give you anything you want. These hellhounds have been dragging me around for three days. I haven't eaten or slept or drank anything in all that time. They're SNIFFER DOGS, with a demonic sense of smell. They can smell their prey from the other side of the city. And their prey is people like you, unaffected by the curse. As long as they're held by the chains they won't attack me, so I can't risk letting them go, but at any moment my strength will give out and then...'

To try to kill the Sniffer Dogs, turn to **419**. To use smoke-oil on them, turn to **432**. To use a magic potion, if you have any, turn to **444**.

408

You are at the base of the watchtower on top of the cliff. The huge broken statue of the goddess Sindla stands nearby. Next to the watchtower is a ruined guardhouse, a small temple and a few newly built wooden huts. There is smoke coming out through the chimney of one of the huts. Four tracks lead from the settlement into the gloom and an old signpost points the way down each one. You read the signs – North Foraging Path, West Foraging Path, Corpse Road, The Well.

To go into the hut, turn to **125**. To go into the watchtower, turn to **79**. To take the north foraging path, turn to **8**. To take the west foraging path, turn to **23**. To take the path to the well, turn to **54**. To take the Corpse Road, turn to **198**.

Sinna grips your arm with a trembling hand. He has a look of horror on his face.

'If I had known the price that must be paid,' he gasps, 'I don't think I would have had the courage to do what needs to be done. If you truly wish to be killed by the giants then I have something that will help you. It is called Weakwater...'

He struggles to pull something from a pouch and gives it to you. It is a small vial of colourless liquid.

'I use it on my enemies,' he explains. 'I slip it in their drink and it makes them lose all their fighting skill. Take it... Use it if you must...'

You may drink the Weakwater now or later. If you do so it will reduce your *SKILL* score to 2 points.

You stand up and bid Sinna farewell. There is nothing you can do for him now. To grab one of the rings, turn to **356**. To leave the cavern and go back to the refectory, turn to **460**.

You and Brother Tobyn follow the strange red-eyed man through the crowd away from the approaching guards. You're careful where you tread; the streets are filthy with rubbish and droppings. Nasty-looking villains of every type hang out on each corner you pass: cut-purses, hired killers looking for work, disgraced minor wizards down on their luck, smugglers selling poison and stolen jewellery ... but they all seem wary of the man in the grey robes and leave the three of you alone.

Brother Tobyn is struggling to keep up. He's short of breath, his wound is hurting him and he's sweating. You let him lean on you as you carry on.

Rising above the houses ahead of you are massive walls, and behind them is a forbidding building topped by two towers, from the taller of which a standard flaps in the wind, showing a dragon and a pirate ship.

'You don't want to go anywhere near there,' says the red-eyed man. 'That is Lord Azzur's palace.'

You've heard tales of Varek Azzur – nightmare tales – and you hope you can leave Port Blacksand without having any dealings with the sinister ex-pirate who rules the city.

Soon you come to Catfish River that runs through the town and is the main source of the great stink that hangs over the place. You see sewage, dead animals and dead fish floating in it. And there – the body of a woman drifting past with three rats perched on her back. Nobody else pays it any attention.

Your guide stops. You are at a bridge, with a row of stakes along either side of it, each one topped with the skull of some monstrous creature. The wind whistles over the bridge and through the skulls, making a sad, sighing sound, almost like singing. The man mutters something and leads you down some steps to a hut hidden under the bridge. A sign reads Keep Out, but the man ignores it and goes in. Turn to **430**.

You climb through the blackened window of the jeweller's shop ... and come face to face with a demon jeweller hiding in the shadows. He smiles at you, showing a mouth full of gold teeth, and then raises two clawed hands and strikes. You dodge to one side to avoid his attack only to find that the floorboards have been burnt away. You drop like a stone and as you fall you catch a glimpse of several more demons waiting in the cellar below. Turn to **330.**

412

You go into the shop. The light shimmering on the walls is refracted through the bottles and jars of potions into different colours, which is why you don't notice the glowing purple pool in the floor. It opens up beneath your feet and you feel yourself falling. You have been sucked into a demon portal. Turn to **355.**

413

The hours pass slowly. You think you'll never get to sleep but at some point you must do because the next thing you know you're being jolted awake by a movement. You open your eyes and see a terrible sight.

A hideous, ancient demon is looming over you. Completely bald, with rough, warty skin and the same horrible dark eyes as the possessed merchant. It's clearly not as strong as that other demon, but it still has long claws and sharp teeth. It snarls at you, dropping spittle on to your face, and raises a hand to strike.

It's then that you realize it's Brother Tobyn. The infected wound has turned him into a monster of the night. You throw him off and just manage to scuttle away towards the cell door.

The demon thing comes after you on all fours, teeth bared, ready to strike. You get to the door and try to open it...

To cry out for help, turn to **433**. To turn and fight the demon with your bare hands, turn to **53**. If you have a key, do you want to try it? If so, turn to **454**.

414

You open the 'Dragon's Breath' potion bottle and foul-smelling green smoke fills the cellar. Blossom takes in great gulps of it and smiles.

'Oh, what a lovely smell!' she cries. 'It's always good to be wearing an expensive perfume when you're killing and eating someone!'

Cross the 'Dragon's Breath' potion off your Adventure Sheet and turn to **313**.

415

You walk down the street and come to some steps going up. You climb them and find that they lead to a bridge that crosses over a lower street. There's someone lying on the bridge. It's a wounded city guard.

'Go back... And stay away from the south gate,' he says. 'There are demons there and the gates are unsafe. They'll fall on you… Everything is falling… It's the end… And look out above you!'

You glance up and see movement at a high window. And now you see demons creeping into the street below the bridge. To cross the bridge, turn to **435**. To go back the way you came, turn to **395.**

416

You realize you should have chosen the goggles from the adventurer's belongings. The King of the Imps will have burnt them by now. If you have a bottle of 'Nostalgia' or a compass, turn to **459**. Otherwise, turn to **437.**

417

If you have a thieves' skeleton key and want to try it, turn to **441**. If you have the Icefinger Key and want to try it, turn to **429**. If you have 'Dragon's Breath' and want to try it, turn to **455**. To hit the lock with Fossick's axe, turn to **468**. If you don't want to risk it and leave the cottage, turn to **350.**

418

None of the keys you try will open the box. To use the Icefinger Key, if you have it, turn to **445**. To force it open, choose a weapon and turn to **425**. Otherwise add the locked box to your Equipment List and turn to **364.**

Where its buttocks should be are two faces

419

With a groan, the man lets go of the chains and the dogs leap at you. You just have time to choose a weapon and now must fight the three Sniffer Dogs all at the same time.

	SKILL	STAMINA
First SNIFFER DOG	7	6
Second SNIFFER DOG	7	7
Third SNIFFER DOG	8	5

If you win, turn to **188.**

420

As you go to pick up a weapon, a gout of purple smoke erupts from the fireplace and a creature starts to emerge. Because of the smoke you can't see it clearly yet, only enough to tell that it's nearly as tall as the room. It lumbers over to the table, blocking the way to the door that looks like a book. It picks up an axe. And then another ... and another ... and another.

The smoke clears and you see the creature clearly. Even though it has no head it is twice your height, with four arms, two facing forwards and two facing backwards, and in each hand it holds an axe. It is standing with what, in a normal creature, would be its back towards you and where its buttocks should be are two faces, one male and one female. They are both grinning.

To fight the creature, turn to **391**. To run through the door with the moon symbol, turn to **299**. To escape through the door that leads to the Walkway of Evening, turn to **84**. To throw a bottle of smoke-oil at its feet, turn to **371**.

421

Your hand closes on... One of your socks.

It smells of cheese.

Damn.

Your adventure is over.

422

What will you offer Lunara? Check to see what you have in your pack. If you have some cold sausage and want to put it in the dish, turn to **434**. To put an apple in the dish, turn to **57**. To put some dried fish in the dish, turn to **30**.

423

'The Gates of Death are right here under the temple,' says Castrabel. 'That's why the city was made invisible, so nobody could find them and open them. We work here all our lives keeping the city safe, but now Ulrakaah is trying to create enough demons to open the gates. I've never been brave enough to go down and look for them. The old entrance was sealed by a rock fall, but there is a secret tunnel here somewhere in the temple. While I've been praying in here I've heard lots of banging and crashing. I think demons might be trying to break their way through.'

To ask Castrabel where the High Priestess is, turn to **384**. To ask about the temple, turn to **440**. To return to the dormitory, turn to **295**.

424

You dismount and let the horse return to Fossick in the woods before walking along the bottom of the great wall. Soon you come to a group of low buildings. With no more room inside the city, the citizens of Salamonis have had to build new houses out here, huddled hard against the wall. You have only just begun to explore this little village when you see bodies lying in the dirt. There has obviously been a battle of some sort here. You go over for a closer look. The bodies have been horribly clawed and bitten. This must be the work of demons. You will need to be extra careful from now on. You see someone's pack lying half buried under a broken cart. You pull it out and add its contents to your own.

Add the following to your Equipment List: a meal of dried dates that will add 3 *STAMINA* points whenever you choose to eat them, a purse of 3 Gold Pieces, and a jar of healing ointment.

It feels risky here outside the city walls. You hurry back to the gates, and then carry on through.

You find a small square on the other side, with a customs house, an inn and a stable block. There is no sign of life, apart from a familiar black carriage that has stopped by the customs house. The driver is attending to the horses and watches warily as you dismount and knock the dust from your clothing.

Turn to **200.**

425

You jam the end of your chosen weapon into the lock and try to force it open. There's a snap, a click, a whirring sound, and then your weapon shatters into a thousand pieces.

'You should be more careful,' says Swann. (Remove the weapon from your Equipment List.)

Before you can reply, the box shakes and rattles, and then fold itself in half, and then in half again … and again and again and again until it disappears in a puff of smoke. When the smoke clears there's only a small blue frog sitting on the counter. It looks at you, croaks, and jumps into your pocket. Turn to **364.**

426

You open the 'Collywobbles' potion bottle and a nasty brown gas explodes out of it. Blossom breathes some in and suddenly looks very sick.

'Oo-er,' she says. 'I'm not feeling too well.' She clutches her stomach and lets out an almighty burp that shakes dust down from the floorboards above you, and then lets out another one, and then an explosive fart and finally the biggest, loudest belch you've ever heard, as she expels the demon spirit from her body.

The DISEMBODIED DEMON SPIRIT crouches there, part reptile, part dog, part shade and all angry.

'You'll pay for this,' it snarls and scurries towards you. You quickly choose a weapon and defend yourself.

DEMON SPIRIT   *SKILL 5*   *STAMINA 6*

You can only harm the Demon Spirit if you are armed with a magical weapon. If you do not have a magical weapon you cannot hope to win this fight. However, if you are using a magical weapon, and you win, turn to **458.**

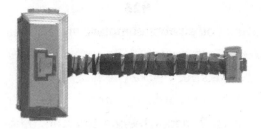

427

There's no sign of the city from here, only a view across the Plain of Bronze. You explore the top of the rock and can't find any way down, but see that its surface is riddled with small holes each about the width of a finger. As you crouch down to inspect one of them more closely, something pokes out of it, like a pink tentacle. You look around you; there are more tentacles coming out from all over the rock. You have landed on a nest of rock worms. They nose out blindly, swaying as if dancing, and before you know it one of them has wrapped around your ankle. You try to peel it off but another one wraps around your wrist, and another... Soon you are trapped in a web of worms that holds you tight.

Now a much bigger worm emerges from a large hole near the centre of the red rock. And this one has a mouth. You are worm food.

If you have a bottle of 'Nostalgia' or a compass, turn to **459**. Otherwise, turn to **437**.

428

You walk down the street. There are shops on both sides – a swordsmith, a carpenter, a tailor – but most of them have been boarded up. One of them, a jeweller's, has been gutted by fire and you catch a glimpse of something golden glinting in the darkness. Finally, you come to a shop with a sign hanging outside it in the shape of a scroll. It says 'Sandford Swann. Mapmaker.' There's a light burning inside. You peer through the window and see a large man wearing a full-face helmet, and with him are four heavily-armed Man-Orcs.

To enter the map shop, turn to **393**. To go into the jeweller's, turn to **411**. To turn around and go back up to the crossroads and try another street, turn to **108.**

429

You put the key into the lock and turn it. Instantly a searing heat burns up your arm and the next moment your clothes are on fire. You rush out into the night, hoping that the rain will douse the flames. But this is magic fire. Nothing can stop it burning.

Your adventure is over.

430

Once inside the hut, the man locks the door and throws off his grey robes, somehow changing completely. Gone are the red eyes and reptilian skin, and instead, standing before you is an old man dressed all in white, with long white hair and a long white beard.

'Forgive the disguise,' he says, getting some jars down from a shelf. 'I don't like to show my hand. I try to stay away from other people, but when I heard there was a Guardian from the Crucible Isles here with his young acolyte, I had to find you. My name is Nicodemus and I know what your mission is – to stop the demon plague. It threatens everyone in Allansia and it is only a matter of time before it spreads to the rest of Titan. That cannot be allowed to happen. I will help you get your smoke-oil to the High Priestess at the Temple of Throff. I cannot come with you, alas, as I never leave this place any more, but I have magic potions that will aid you on your quest...'

He sets the potion jars out in front of you. Each one contains a different coloured liquid. You read the labels and wonder what they might do.

'Take these four,' he says. 'Any more than that and there is a risk they will react with each other and destroy you. You can use each one only once. Simply open the bottle and release the magic. Each one is powerful against a different threat, but I cannot tell you which one to use when; you must let the goddess guide your hand.'

Add the following magic potions to your Equipment List: 'Thick as Thieves', 'Pretty as a Picture', 'Collywobbles' and 'Dragon's Breath'.

As you put the jars in your pack, Nicodemus examines Brother Tobyn, who is slumped in a chair, his whole body trembling, his skin turning grey.

'The wound is infected,' says Nicodemus. 'It is only a matter of time before he turns into a demon. You will have to travel alone.'

You are about to protest when Brother Tobyn whispers your name.

'Nicodemus is right,' he says, feebly gripping your arm. 'I don't have the strength to walk another step, or to fight the demonic infection. Only you can save Titan. Be brave and pure of heart...'

'And be quick,' says Nicodemus. 'The longer you delay, the worse the plague gets. Take Bridge Street to the Market Square and then on to the main gate. From there, take the road to Silverton and on to Salamonis. The people of Salamonis are more civilized than the scum who live here and should be able to tell you how to find the Invisible City. Tell no one of your mission until you are there. And take my robe. It will get you safely out of town. There its magic ends, however; after that – you're on your own.'

He picks up the robe and offers it to you. You smell sulphur coming from it and see a glint in the wizard's eye. Can you trust anyone in this awful place?

If you want to put on the robes, turn to **212**. If you want to attack Nicodemus and try to take more of his potions, turn to **449**. If you want to grab Brother Tobyn and leave without putting on the robes, turn to **369**.

431

You jump down from the hayloft and grab a pitchfork. (Add the pitchfork to your Weapons List.) The Hay Thiever rears up at you and you go in for the kill.

HAY THIEVER   *SKILL 3*   *STAMINA 2*

If you win, turn to **401**.

432

You know how to deal with demons. You take a vial of smoke-oil from your pack, checking how many you have left, and then smash it at the feet of the three Sniffer Dogs. Their huge nostrils suck in the oily gas so quickly that you hardly see it. They yelp in pain and, the next moment, they're writhing on the ground with purple smoke steaming from their mouths.

Soon, the dogs have become three harmless household pooches. They whimper and lick the hands of the man as he falls to his knees, sobbing. Turn to **188.**

433

Responding to your cries for help, the dungeon-master comes running. His face appears at the barred window and he cackles with delight.

'Oh-ho, this should be quite a show,' he crows. 'But we don't want things to be too one-sided, do we? No fun if it's over too quickly. Here – take your pick.'

He thrusts his hands through the bars. In one he holds a vial of your smoke-oil, and in the other he has a rusty old bread knife. To take the smoke-oil, turn to **6**. To take the rusty bread knife, turn to **26**.

434

You put a piece of sausage in the bowl and send a prayer to Lunara to help you find the priestess, apologizing that your offering is not greater. Nothing happens. Turn to **406**.

435

You step on to the bridge and there's a sudden screech from above. A demon has thrown itself out of the window. It knocks you off the bridge. Turn to **330**.

The demonic army charges forward like a tide of filth

436

You take hold of one of the gigantic rings. It takes all of your strength to turn it. You hear the squeal of metal scraping against metal, and finally there's a THUNK as the gates open. You pull them slowly back, releasing a foul stench of sulphur and rotting meat and excrement. Ahead of you is a cavern similar to the one you are in, with weirdly-coloured crystals glowing in its walls. On the ground are heaps of dead bodies. You hear a frightful buzzing sound and see a black cloud streaming towards you. You cover your mouth and nose and the next moment the cloud is upon you. It is made up of ten thousand flies that swarm around you, biting your face and hands. You swipe at them but now see that they are the least of your worries, for behind the flies comes an army. An army of dead things, monstrous things, twisted things, hopping, crawling, flapping and squirming. You see huge tusked beasts with ghouls riding on their backs wielding cruel barbed weapons and screaming with laughter. You see demon soldiers, warped by the curse of Chaos, wearing rusted armour and chanting the name of Ulrakaah. You see giant insects and deformed Lizardmen, bat things and rat things and nameless creatures from your nightmares, half bird, half fish.

Behind them walks a creature so tall its great head,

wearing a horned helmet, almost touches the roof. This was once a woman, but she has grown huge and vile by feasting on the demonic energies of this realm. She crouches slightly, with a bent back, and is wielding two massive swords, one in each hand. Her face is the face of death, with rotting flesh, sharpened teeth and pitiless dead eyes. She sees you and laughs, the sound echoing inside your skull.

So this is Ulrakaah, Queen of Darkness, Mother of Demons, and you have released her back into the world. She raises her swords triumphantly, opens her mouth and shrieks…

'Ulrakaaaah!'

And suddenly the demonic army charges forward like a tide of filth and rolls over you. The last thing you see before you die is one of Ulrakaah's swords slashing down through the fetid air to hack at you.

 Your adventure is over.

437

You are so close, but still so far. You will never find the Invisible City.

Your adventure is over.

438

You smash a bottle of smoke-oil on the cellar floor and release its contents. The weird yellow gas finds its way to Blossom and shoots straight up her nose. She squeals and clutches her throat, falling to the floor where she writhes about, coughing and choking, purple smoke billowing out of her mouth. Finally she goes into a back-breaking spasm, then becomes rigid as a plank of wood, before giving a shriek and flopping in a heap.

'What have you done to her?' shouts Fossick, who has been watching from the trapdoor. 'If she's harmed, I'll kill you!'

You go over to Blossom, fearing the worst, but see, with relief, that she's back to normal. Turn to **458.**

439

'The most important thing to remember about the Gates of Death is that you must never try to open them or you will allow Ulrakaah's demonic army back into this realm where they will be ten times stronger than in their own realm. I do not know how to pass safely through the gates to confront them on the other side. There is a book here, in the library, though, that will give you the information you seek, *The Book of Death*. I can, however, tell you what magic you will need to defeat Ulrakaah.'

To ask the Holy Man what magic you will need, turn to **402**. To ask about Ulrakaah, turn to **452**. To return to the tunnel, turn to **147**.

440

'There is a balance in everything,' says Castrabel. 'Between day and night, between left and right, between chaos and order. You cannot have one without the other. Throff tries to keep the balance in the universe, and there is a balance here. This temple is symmetrical. It has a light side and a dark side. The north side is a mirror image of the south side and the Temple of Throff is at the centre.'

To ask Castrabel where the High Priestess is, turn to **384**. To ask about the Gates of Death, turn to **423**. To return to the dormitory, turn to **295**.

441

You put the key into the lock and turn it. Instantly a searing heat burns up your arm, but the dragon's jaws part and the lock snaps open.

Inside you can see all of Fossick's treasure – but a powerful acid is dissolving it. You just have time to snatch out two items: a jewelled warhammer and a Harp of Healing. You have seen a harp like this before. (If you ever lose a fight, the harp will restore 8 *STAMINA* points to you, but only once.)

There is nothing else for you here, so you leave the woodman's cottage. Turn to **350**.

442

Your hand closes on the bottle of 'Nostalgia'. You pop the cork from its neck. A smell of pears wafts out and you feel your whole world spinning... Time seems to run backwards... You realize the potion will allow you to relive part of your adventure... Turn to **14**.

443

You go through the door and find yourself in a toilet, turned purple by the light from a demon portal in the floor. Someone has scratched a message into the wall: 'Sinna was here. He bathed his blade in magic potion.' To try to jump over the portal, turn to **342**. To return to the passageway, turn to **279**.

444

The Sniffer Dogs are straining at their chains. The poor man's arms are trembling. You have to deal with this quickly before he lets go.

To use a 'Thick as Thieves' potion, turn to **456**. To use a 'Pretty as a Picture' potion, turn to **467**. To use the 'Dragon's Breath' potion, turn to **85**. To use the 'Collywobbles' potion, turn to **65**. To use some 'Nostalgia' perfume, turn to **10**.

If you have none of these, you will have to fight the hounds, turn to **419**.

445

You take out the key you found in the prisoner's boot in the dungeons at Port Blacksand and slip it into the lock. It works. The box snaps open and inside you find 20 Gold Pieces, a silver compass and a jar of 'Pretty as a Picture' potion.

Add the items to your Equipment List and turn to **364**.

446

You sit there, picking flies out of your teeth and looking up at the high city walls of Salamonis. They must have stood here for hundreds of years and seen countless people come and go. They're built from massive blocks of ancient, weathered stone and look like they could hold back an army of giants.

You look down to where the road passes through them and are surprised to see nobody guarding the gates. To explore the area outside the walls, turn to **424**. To enter through the gates, turn to **200**.

447

Nothing grows up here and you can see nothing below but the endless dead expanse of the plain. There is certainly no sign of any city. You look for a way off the rock but can't find any safe way of getting down from the summit. If you have a bottle of 'Nostalgia' or a compass, then turn to **459**. Otherwise you are stuck here, turn to **437**.

448

You carry on down the road. If you have a trowel, turn to **98**. If not turn to **428.**

449

Only a born fool attacks a wizard as powerful as Nicodemus. Before you've even taken two steps towards him he curses you and casts a spell.

You turn into a goldfish and Nicodemus drops you into the Catfish River.

Your adventure is over.

450

You take out all your precious vials of smoke-oil and hand them over to Denka. She looks at them for a moment, and then smiles. Slowly her smile grows wider and wider until her face seems to be splitting open.

'Oh, Queen Ulrakaah will be so pleased,' she hisses, and her eyes begin to glow purple. 'You are a fool. To have come this far only to fail now!' She laughs and hurls all the vials to the floor. There is the sound of breaking glass and the room is filled with purple gas. You see the shape of Denka shifting inside the purple cloud.

'The effects of smoke-oil are reversed on demons that have taken on human form,' she purrs. 'Now, see me as I truly am!'

You watch as her ears become big and pointed and her teeth grow long and sharp. She rises towards the ceiling, her robes dropping away, and before your eyes she turns into a giant, hairless cat, standing up on its rear legs.

'Now you must die!' she howls, raising a paw armed with vicious claws the size of daggers.

And so you must fight DENKA MANSELL.

DENKA   *SKILL 8*   *STAMINA 8*

If you win, turn to **233**. If you lose, turn to **255**.

451

You know that these creatures will steal anything. Perhaps if you can find its lair there will be treasures in it. It moves slowly, its tentacles groping ahead of it towards the back of the barn where there's a gap at the bottom of the boards. It crawls out and there's just room for you to wriggle after it.

It's stopped raining and the moon is out, but there are puddles everywhere. You're wet and filthy from crawling but are so intent on following the Hay Thief that you hardly notice. It goes over to a crumbling wall and enters a hole between two stones.

To stick your hand in the hole, turn to **278**. To give up and go back to the hayloft, turn to **401**.

452

'Ulrakaah, Queen of Darkness, lives in the realm of death beyond the gates. She can only be defeated by using a combination of magic and one of her enchanted khopesh blades. I can supply you with most of the magic you need, the khopesh you will have to find yourself, if you do not already carry one. I know there is one here somewhere in the temple, however.'

To ask the Holy Man what magic you will need, turn to **402**. To ask about the Gates of Death, turn to **439**. To go back out through the hole, turn to **147**.

453

You raise your khopesh and prepare to take on the Demon Horde. There are a huge number of them, and they are far more powerful than you, but you are pure of heart... and armed with a blade as sharp as a razor! The khopesh is an enchanted weapon that was made for Ulrakaah herself, and is enormously powerful against her underlings.

You raise the khopesh, pointing it towards the roof. It glows with a purple light and instantly the *SKILL* and *STAMINA* of the Demon Horde are reduced to a tenth of their power (simply remove the 0 from the end of the two attributes.)

Now you can do battle with them. If you win, turn to **105**. If you lose, turn to **60**.

454

You take the key out of your boot and desperately search for the keyhole in the door ... and that's when you remember that cell doors only have keyholes on the outside... And now you feel something tearing at the back of your tunic.

While you've been distracted, Brother Tobyn has attacked you, and you feel a trickle of blood crawling down your skin. (Lose 2 *STAMINA* points.) To call for help, turn to **433**. To try to fight the demon with your bare hands, turn to **53**.

455

You take a jar of 'Dragon's Breath' out of your pack and pull out the cork. A cloud of noxious green gas seeps out. The stink is awful. Your eyes are streaming and you want to be sick, but you force yourself to watch as the gas curls around the lock, then rises up to form a cloud over the chest. Slowly the cloud forms into letters spelling out a message...

'Magic has frozen the dragon's jaws,
Only magic words will make them thaw,
Without the spell then do not try,
Or the dragon's curse will make you fry.'

To try to open the chest regardless, turn to **417**. To leave the Dwarf's cottage, turn to **350**.

456

You pull the cork out of the jar labelled 'Thick as Thieves' and hideous blue smoke wafts out. You cover your mouth and nose and drop the bottle. The smoke seems to be alive. It seeks out the Sniffer Dogs and they can't help but breathe it in... If this is your first attempt at using a magic potion, turn to **45**. If this is your second attempt, turn to **27**. If this is your third attempt, turn to **419**.

457

You walk deeper into the cavern, trying not to think about how strange and unnatural this all is. You come to an archway of rock and walk through it into an even bigger cavern where you see the remains of an ancient building, perhaps a temple, half buried by rocks. You see ruined pillars and walkways, cloisters, buttresses, and, in the centre, a huge pit of purple fire.

The cavern looks deserted, but as you walk towards the fire pit you see movement. Demon soldiers have appeared on a high walkway. They jeer down at you and throw filth, and, as they do so, more demons appear, from holes in the walls and cracks in the ground, from tunnels and caves and ruined doorways. Their armour and weapons are rusty, their flesh decaying, many are missing limbs ... but there are hundreds of them. An army. And alongside them, emerging from the shadows, are other creatures, dead things, monstrous things, twisted things, hopping, crawling, flapping, squirming. You see giant insects and deformed Lizardmen, and nameless creatures from your nightmares, half bird, half fish. Several huge tusked beasts lumber in to block the way back to the gates. The ghouls riding on their backs are wielding cruel, barbed weapons and screaming with laughter.

Hearing the ghouls, all the monsters now start to laugh

and chant, louder and louder... 'Ulrakaaah! Ulrakaaah! Ulrakaah!' Some turn their naked behinds towards you, other spit and curse, some just stare in silence, sharpening their blades.

And now, from the fiery pit in the middle of the cavern floor, something monstrously huge begins to rise up... You see two great twisted horns, and then a helmet, and then a face that you know you will never forget as long as you live ... which might not be that long at all. This was once a woman, but she now has the face of death. The teeth are yellow and pointed like the teeth of a cat. The flesh, which is peeling and rotten, is a corpse-like bluish grey. The eyes burn with a red fire of hatred.

And still the figure rises up ... and up, and up, and up until its head almost touches the roof. And now this awful thing tilts back its head and lets out a terrible shriek...

'Uuuuurrrrrrraaaaaaaawwwwwwwwwrrrrrrr...'

You realize it is calling out its own name. This is Ulrakaah, Queen of Darkness, Mother of Demons. She who was once a beautiful high priestess of Throff has grown huge and vile by feasting on the demonic energies of this realm.

'Who is this who has come into my realm uninvited?' she howls, staring at you. 'Like a slug from a midden heap? Well, we shall show this scrap of nothing, this fleck of dung, our hospitality, shan't we, my little children, my dear ones?'

She laughs at you, the sound echoing inside your skull, and raises two massive swords, one in each hand, while her horde caper and scream and howl all around her.

'I will give you the gift of death,' she says and now her army marches towards you. There are so many of them, with more pouring in from the caves and tunnels on every side. It is going to be a hard battle to win.

Make a note of the attributes for the DEMON HORDE:

DEMON HORDE   *SKILL 400*   *STAMINA 800*

If you ate some of the Holy Man's Seeds of Galana before passing through the gates, turn to **168**. If not, turn to **25**.

458

You have rid Blossom of the demon spirit. She sits up, blinking and confused.

'Well done!' shouts Fossick from the trapdoor. 'You've saved my beautiful Blossom. Come on up and I'll give you your reward.'

He lowers down a ladder, and you and Blossom climb out of the cellar. Fossick hugs you both and leads you over to his treasure chest.

'You can choose three things from in here,' he says and then waves his hands over a strange dragon-shaped lock while muttering a magic spell... 'Unctus fibaris nostratum...' The dragon's jaws widen and the lock clicks open.

Inside you see all of Fossick's treasure. Choose any three of the following items: a bag of 10 Gold Pieces, a jewelled warhammer, a Deathstone, a Horn of Plenty, a Harp of Healing, a Hero's Medallion.

Turn to **290**.

459

You use your magic item, delete it from your Equipment List, and travel back in time. Turn to **466**.

460

You are in a room with a long table down the middle of it. This must be the refectory where the temple workers eat. There are two doors here, one leading to the dormitory and one with images of cooking implements carved into it. There is also an opening in the east wall where someone – or something – has smashed a hole through the brickwork.

To investigate the hole in the wall, turn to **195**. To go back into the dormitory, turn to **295**. To go through the door with the images of cooking implements carved into it, turn to **273**.

461

You undress, slip into the warm, soothing water and feel instantly revived. This is no ordinary bath. (Restore your *STAMINA* score to its Initial level and add 1 to your *SKILL* score.) Afterwards, you quickly dress and return to the passageway. Turn to **279**.

462

You stare at the compass, the pointer spinning round and round and round ... and all around you grows dark, until all there is in the universe is that hand spinning for ever ... and then that too dims.

Your adventure is over.

463

You climb up on to the Lamassu's back and take hold of the thick black hair growing at the base of its neck. It runs along, faster and faster, then unfolds its wings, beats them, once, twice, three times, gives a great kick and rises into the air. A few more beats pull it up into the sky. You feel its powerful muscles working beneath you.

Up and up it goes until you can see all of the countryside between Silverton and Salamonis spread out like a map. Soon you are flying over Salamonis itself. From up here everything looks calm and peaceful. The Lamassu follows the road and it's not long before you see the Moonstone Hills to the east. The hills form a barrier between western and eastern Allansia and from way up here they don't look very big at all. Snaking through the centre of the hills is Trolltooth Pass: the only way into northwest Allansia from the Flatlands and beyond.

The Lamassu's strong wings flap and thrum the air as on you fly. Day fades into night and you fall asleep, holding tight to the Lamassu's hair, safe in the knowledge that it won't drop you. When you awake, the sun is sending its first fiery rays over the horizon and you are flying high above the Flatlands, an endless, featureless expanse of grassy steppes. You press southwards and, when the sun is high in the sky, grass gives way to rocky scrubland. You are on the fringes of the Plain of Bronze. It looks dead and desolate, a windswept patchwork of sand and ash and lumps of bronze that reflect the sunlight back in flashes.

'They say that there was once a great battle here,' says the Lamassu, 'during the War of the Wizards. And there was a terrible fire, like a fallen sun, that burnt to dust what had been a rich and fertile plain. The stories tell that the Invisible City is somewhere in the middle, near where there are three pillars known as the Three Tiger Mountains, though each is only really a tall column of rock. One is named Mount Rogaar, after the lion god. One is named Mount Magir, after the tiger god, and the third is named after their sister, Meerar, goddess of cats. They say that you can see the Invisible City from the top of one of the three peaks, if you know how to look. I could set you down there, but I have no idea what you will see. And we must be quick, for there is danger all around.'

As the Lamassu says this, you see that what you at first took for a dark cloud in the distance is moving fast towards you, and as it gets nearer you see that it is actually a flock of birds. But they're no ordinary birds. They have been cursed by the demon plague and are so mutated and malformed you wonder how they can still fly. Some have massive, clacking beaks, others have huge dragon-like claws, some have steel-tipped feathers.

You can see no signs of any city, but below you, you can now see three tall columns of rock standing alone, each one a different colour. One is reddish brown, one is sandy-coloured and one is ash grey. The top of each rock is only about twenty paces wide.

To land on the red rock, turn to **266**. To land on the sandy one, turn to **280**. To land on the grey one, turn to **297**. To return to Salamonis and seek more information in the city, turn to **354**.

464

You inspect the adventurer's box. If you have the Icefinger Key, turn to **445**. If you want to try any other key you have, turn to **418**. If you want to force the lock, choose a weapon and turn to **425**.

465

You walk down the street, which comes to a dead end. There's a shop here, though, with a sign saying: Magic Artefacts. You can see coloured lights glinting inside, red and blue and purple. There are some broken jars of potion near the doorway, and when you look closer you see that one of them isn't broken after all. It's a jar of 'Pretty as a Picture'. (Add the potion to your Equipment List.)

To go into the shop to look for more potions, turn to **412**. To go back the way you came, turn to **395**.

466

If you have any of the following items listed on your Adventure Sheet, cross them off now:

Silver Star Ring, Silver Compass, Flask of Firewater, Silver Trowel, Silver Swift Boots, Sun Hat, Walking Staff, Locked Box, Blue Frog, Bier Goggles, Map, Bronze Star, Bronze Swift Boots, Staff, Canteen, Bronze Compass.

(Your Provisions, Gold Pieces, any potions and vials of smoke-oil are unaffected by the strange magic.)

Restore your *SKILL*, *STAMINA* and *LUCK* scores to their Initial values and turn to **200**.

467

You pull the cork out of the bottle labelled 'Pretty as a Picture' and a cloud of turquoise gas that smells of lavender escapes. The hounds cough and choke. They are weakened but still alive. If this is your first attempt at using a magic potion, turn to **45**. If this is your second attempt, turn to **27**. If this is your third attempt, turn to **419**.

468

You raise the axe and swing with all your might, but as it strikes the lock the treasure chest bursts into flames, and you watch helplessly as it turns to dust and ashes.

The treasure is destroyed. You can do nothing but carry on with your adventure. Turn to **350.**

469

Denka has defeated you. Your adventure is over.

470

You emerge on the other side of the Gates to find your own body lying lifeless on the floor. Quickly you return to it and the next moment you are alive again.

You stand up, wobbly and weak and gasping for breath. You hear a voice thanking you and turn to see Alesstis, holding out her hands towards you. With her are the Fish with a Thousand Voices, Castrabel, the young acolyte, and the Wooden Scribe. They hug you and thank you and press gifts on you – magic potions and gold and enchanted weapons.

'You have saved us and you have saved all Titan,' says the High Priestess. 'You are no longer a mere acolyte. You are now a fully-fledged sorcerer. Together we can make more smoke-oil, enough to cure all the demons that remain in Allansia, and after that I am sure you will do many more extraordinary things and go on many amazing journeys and save many people, and your name will go down in history. Good luck on your adventures and may your stamina never fail.'

HOW TO FIGHT
THE CREATURES OF
THE GATES OF DEATH

Before embarking on your adventure, you must first determine your own strengths and weaknesses.

To see how effective your preparations have been you must use the dice to determine your *SKILL, STAMINA* and *LUCK* scores. On pages 340-341 there is an *Adventure Sheet* which you may use to record the details of an adventure. On it you will find boxes for recording your *SKILL, STAMINA* and *LUCK* scores. Write on the *Adventure Sheet* in pencil so you can erase previous scores when you start again. Or make photocopies of the blank *Adventure Sheet*.

SKILL, STAMINA AND LUCK

To determine your *Initial SKILL, STAMINA* and *LUCK* scores:

- Roll one die. Add 6 to this number and enter this total in the *SKILL* box on the *Adventure Sheet*.
- Roll both dice. Add 12 to the number rolled and enter

this total in the *STAMINA* box.

- Roll one die, add 6 to this number and enter this total in the *LUCK* box.

SKILL reflects your swordsmanship and fighting expertise; the higher the better. *STAMINA* represents your strength; the higher your *STAMINA*, the longer you will survive. *LUCK* represents how lucky a person you are. Luck – and magic – are facts of life in the fantasy world you are about to explore.

SKILL, STAMINA and *LUCK* scores change constantly during an adventure, so keep an eraser handy. You must keep an accurate record of these scores. But never rub out your *Initial* scores. Although you may receive additional *SKILL, STAMINA* and *LUCK* points, these totals may never exceed your Initial scores, except on very rare occasions, when instructed on a particular page.

BATTLES

When you are told to fight a creature, you must resolve the battle as described below. First record the creature's *SKILL* and *STAMINA* scores (as given on the page) in an empty *Monster Encounter Box* on your *Adventure Sheet*. The sequence of combat is then:

1. Roll the two dice for the creature. Add its *SKILL* score.

This total is **its** *Attack Strength*.

2. Roll the two dice for yourself. Add your current *SKILL*. This total is **your** *Attack Strength*.

3. Whose *Attack Strength* is higher? If your *Attack Strength* is higher, you have wounded the creature. If the creature's *Attack Strength* is higher, it has wounded you. (If both are the same, you have both missed – start the next *Attack Round* from step 1 above.)

4. If you wounded the creature, subtract 2 points from its *STAMINA* score. You may use *LUCK* here to do additional damage (see 'Using Luck in Battles' below).

5. If the creature wounded you, subtract 2 points from **your** *STAMINA* score. You may use *LUCK* to minimize the damage (see below).

6. Make the appropriate changes to either the creature's or your own *STAMINA* score (and your *LUCK* score if you used *LUCK)* and begin the next *Attack Round* (repeat steps 1–6).

This continues until the STAMINA score of either you or the creature you are fighting has been reduced to zero (death).

LUCK

Sometimes you will be told to *Test your Luck*. As you will discover, using *LUCK* is a risky business. The way you *Test your Luck* is as follows:

Roll two dice. If the number rolled is *equal to* or *less than* your current *LUCK* score, you have been *lucky*. If the number rolled is *higher* than your current *LUCK* score, you have been *unlucky*. The consequences of being *lucky* or *unlucky* will be found on the page.

Each time you *Test your Luck,* you must subtract one point from your current *LUCK* score. So the more you rely on luck, the more risky this becomes.

Using Luck in Battles

In battles, you always have the option of using your luck either to score a more serious wound on a creature, or to minimize the effects of a wound the creature has just scored on you.

If you have just wounded the creature: you may *Test your Luck* as described above. If you are *lucky,* subtract an *extra* 2 points from the creature's *STAMINA* score (i.e. 4 instead of 2 normally). But if you are *unlucky,* you must restore 1 point to the creature's *STAMINA* (so instead of scoring the normal 2 points of damage, you have now scored only 1).

If the creature has just wounded you: you can *Test your Luck* to try to minimize the wound. If you are *lucky,* restore

1 point of your *STAMINA* (ie. instead of doing 2 points of damage it has done only 1). If you are *unlucky,* subtract 1 *extra STAMINA* point.

Don't forget to subtract 1 point from your *LUCK* score each time you *Test your Luck.*

RESTORING SKILL, STAMINA AND LUCK

Skill

Occasionally, a page may give instructions to alter your SKILL score. A Magic Weapon may increase your SKILL, but remember that only one weapon can be used at a time! You cannot claim 2 SKILL bonuses for carrying two Magic Swords. Your SKILL score can never exceed its Initial value unless specifically instructed.

Stamina and Provisions

Your *STAMINA* score will change a lot during the adventure. As you near your goal, your *STAMINA* level may become dangerously low and battle may be particularly risky, so be careful!

You do not start the game with any Provisions but you may acquire some during the course of your adventure.

If you do, keep track of how many meals you have left by using the Provisions box on the Adventure Sheet. You may eat only one meal at a time. When you eat a meal, add 4 to your *STAMINA* score and deduct 1 point from your Provisions.

You may also restore *STAMINA* points by treating your wounds using the contents of jars of healing ointment. If you have been wounded in battle, and you have some healing ointment, you may use one jar to restore up to 4 *STAMINA* points. You may use only one jar of healing ointment at a time, which must then be discarded.

Don't forget that your *STAMINA* score may never exceed its Initial value unless specifically instructed in the text.

Luck

You will find additions to your *LUCK* score awarded when you have been particularly lucky. Remember that, as with *SKILL* and *STAMINA*, your *LUCK* score may never exceed its Initial value unless specifically instructed on a page.

EQUIPMENT AND POTIONS

You start your adventure without a weapon of any kind, the hardy travelling clothes of an acolyte of the Crucible Isles, and a backpack, in which you can store items you find as your adventure progresses.

During the course of your quest you may well acquire various potions. These should be recorded in the Potions box on your Adventure Sheet.

You may well also find various weapons that you can use. If you find a weapon, write it down in the Weapons box on your Adventure Sheet. Until you acquire a weapon, you must fight unarmed. When you are fighting unarmed, in combat you must reduce your Attack Strength by 2 points and if you injure an enemy you will only cause them 1 point of *STAMINA* damage.

WEAPONS

There are a number of different weapons that you may come across during your adventure and their different qualities are listed below.

NO WEAPON: If you have to fight unarmed you must reduce your Attack Strength by 2 points and any successful hits will only cause your opponent 1 *STAMINA* point of damage.

RUSTY BREADKNIFE: The rusty blade of the breadknife will cause 1 *STAMINA* point of damage on a successful strike.

FIRE IRON: This improvised weapon will cause an enemy 2 *STAMINA* points of damage but wielding it in battle reduces your Attack Strength by 1 point.

PITCHFORK: When used in combat the pitchfork causes 2 *STAMINA* points of damage at a successful hit. However, it was designed for farming, not for battle, and so you must reduce your Attack Strength in battle by 1 point for as long as you are using it.

CUDGEL: A hit from the cudgel causes 2 *STAMINA* points of damage, unless you roll a double whilst calculating your Attack Strength, in which case it will only cause 1 *STAMINA* point of damage.

CLEAVER: This chopping blade will cause 2 *STAMINA* points of damage when used as a weapon.

HARPOON: The harpoon causes 2 *STAMINA* points of damage at a successful strike.

SNEAKY SWORD: This weapon, favoured by thieves, causes 2 *STAMINA* points of damage.

ASSASSIN'S STILETTO: This slim dagger, favoured by hired killers, causes 2 *STAMINA* points of damage. However, the blade is poisoned, so for the first two battles you fight using it, once you have wounded your opponent they will lose 1 *STAMINA* point every Attack Round, regardless of whether you actually strike them or not. After two battles there will not be any more poison left on the blade.

WOODMAN'S AXE: A successful hit with the axe will cause 2 *STAMINA* points of damage. However, if you roll a double whilst calculating your Attack Strength, and you win the Attack Round, its heavy blade will cause 3 *STAMINA* points of damage instead.

TEMPLE GUARD'S AXE: This blessed weapon will cause 2 *STAMINA* points of damage at a successful strike, unless you roll a double whilst calculating your Attack Strength, in which case it will cause 3 *STAMINA* points of damage. As long as you are wielding this weapon in battle you may add 1 point to your Attack Strength.

JEWELLED WARHAMMER: This magical weapon causes 2 *STAMINA* points of damage unless it is used against Demons, in which case it will cause 3 *STAMINA* points of damage. It is also particularly effective against creatures made of stone or crystal. If you make a successful strike against such a creature it will suffer 4 points of *STAMINA* damage!

KHOPESH: The khopesh adds 1 point to your Attack Strength in battle and causes 2 *STAMINA* points of damage at a successful strike. However, when you are fighting Demons it adds 2 points to your Attack Strength and will cause 3 *STAMINA* points of damage.

ADVENTURE SHEET

SKILL

STAMINA

LUCK

EQUIPMENT

GOLD

POTIONS

WEAPONS

PROVISIONS

MONSTER ENCOUNTERS

MONSTER:

SKILL =

STAMINA =

MONSTER:

SKILL =

STAMINA =

MONSTER:

SKILL =

STAMINA =

MONSTER:

SKILL =

STAMINA =

MONSTER:

SKILL =

STAMINA =

MONSTER:

SKILL =

STAMINA =

MONSTER:

SKILL =

STAMINA =

MONSTER:

SKILL =

STAMINA =

MONSTER:

SKILL =

STAMINA =

MONSTER:

SKILL =

STAMINA =

MONSTER:

SKILL =

STAMINA =

MONSTER:

SKILL =

STAMINA =

ADVENTURE SHEET

SKILL

STAMINA

LUCK

EQUIPMENT

GOLD

POTIONS

WEAPONS

PROVISIONS

MONSTER ENCOUNTERS

MONSTER: SKILL = STAMINA =	MONSTER: SKILL = STAMINA =
MONSTER: SKILL = STAMINA =	MONSTER: SKILL = STAMINA =
MONSTER: SKILL = STAMINA =	MONSTER: SKILL = STAMINA =
MONSTER: SKILL = STAMINA =	MONSTER: SKILL = STAMINA =
MONSTER: SKILL = STAMINA =	MONSTER: SKILL = STAMINA =
MONSTER: SKILL = STAMINA =	MONSTER: SKILL = STAMINA =

DEATHTRAP
DUNGEON

IAN
LIVINGSTONE

YOU, the hero, must enter the trap-filled and monster-infested labyrinth of Fang, where YOU must take part in evil Baron Sukumvit's Trial of Champions. Competing against five other adventurers, YOU must discover the key to escaping and winning the Trial.

CREATURE
— OF —
HAVOC

STEVE
JACKSON

**YOU, the hero, must find a way of defeating the feared
necromancer Zharradan Marr. Access the Galleykeep,
Marr's flying vessel, to destroy his portal and his means of
entering Allansia — or perish in the attempt!**

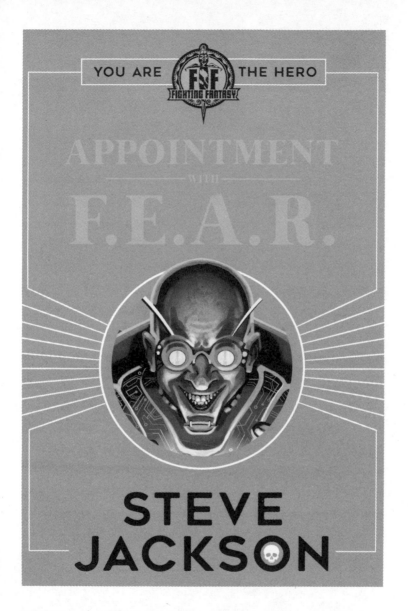

YOU ARE THE HERO

FIGHTING FANTASY

APPOINTMENT

— WITH —

F.E.A.R.

STEVE
JACKSON

YOU are the Silver Crusader. YOU use your superpowers
to discover the location of a top-secret F.E.A.R. meeting,
capture the Titanium Cyborg and his gang, and bring
them to justice and save Titan City. Can YOU complete this
difficult quest?

SORCERY!
THE
SHAMUTANTI HILLS

STEVE JACKSON

YOU, the hero, must search for the legendary Crown of Kings, and journey the Shamutanti Hills. Alive with evil creatures, lawless wanderers and bloodthirsty monsters, the land is riddled with tricks and traps waiting for YOU. **Will YOU be able to cross the hills safely?**

YOU ARE THE HERO

FIGHTING FANTASY

COLLECT THEM ALL, BRAVE ADVENTURER!

CREATURE OF HAVOC — STEVE JACKSON

DEATHTRAP DUNGEON — IAN LIVINGSTONE

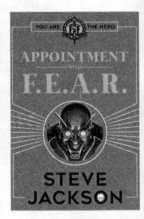

APPOINTMENT WITH F.E.A.R. — STEVE JACKSON

ISLAND OF THE LIZARD KING — IAN LIVINGSTONE

SORCERY! THE SHAMUTANTI HILLS — STEVE JACKSON

THE GATES OF DEATH — STEVE JACKSON / IAN LIVINGSTONE — CHARLIE HIGSON